The Empty Sword

The Empty Sword Saga, Volume 1

Jonathan Zobel

Published by Jonathan Zobel, 2023.

THE EMPTY SWORD

First edition. July 9, 2023.

ISBN: 979-8223789901

Written by Jonathan Zobel.

To my parents who encouraged me to follow my love of storytelling. My test readers who helped me build this series with their feedback and ideas. And the Kelly family and everyone at my church for encourging me as I neared my goal of publishing this book.

Thank you all for everything you've done to help me!

NORTHERN RANGE
ARETOF
THE FROZEN LANDS
ICELIC
LAKE OF ICE
BOILING LAKE
GREEN RIVER
FRUNIET
FOREST LAKE
PRANIAT
UNKNOWN LANDS
GREEN RIVER
TAEDUT
THE SHADOWED PLAINS
THE RUINS OF CURIT
WELLOP
THE DUSKY SEA
THE BLACK PEAK
JEATUT
ICE RIVER
GADWAR
SKYTOP LAKE
ALTUM RUINS
ALTUMI
TIBUT
THE WORLD OF LULANDAL

Pronunciation Guide

Kittrian. KIT-tree-an
Hannela. Han-EH-la
Geltian. Gel-TEE-an
Wheelat. WHEEL-at
Velien. Vel-EEN
Herett. Hair-ET
Lulandal. LUE-lun-doll
Barit. BEAR-it
Areiop. ARE-ee-op
Clydesat. CLYDE-sat
Tredut. TRAY-dut
Talrit. TALL-rit
Fruniet. FROON-ee-et
Annalio. ANN-al-leo
Groman. GROW-man
Blakmian. BLOKE-me-an
Trodontian. Tro-DON-tea-an
Falamore. FAL-la-more
Windmere. WIND-mere
Vulant. Vu-LANT
Lapik. LAY-pick
Prariat. PRAYER-ee-at
Galent. Gay-LENT
Trakken. TRA-ken

Saralia. Sa-RAIL-lee-ah
Altimi. ALL-ti-me
Unkarian. Un-KAR-ee-an
Thaliton. THAL-eh-ton
Amronian. Am-RON-ee-an
Bomski. Bomb-ski
Felinad. Fell-EE-nad

Chapter 1. The Hidden Trail.

"I can't believe you actually talked me into doing this!" Stephen grumbled. He looked up and saw his twin sister look back at him with an annoyed expression as they pushed through the overgrown trail.

"I thought you wanted to do something exciting instead of sitting on that old sofa and reading all day," Victoria retorted in a huff. She pushed aside a shrub and then ducked under a tree branch.

"I did. But getting us lost in this forsaken forest is not what I had in mind," Stephen growled. He pushed a heavy branch out of his way, only to be smacked in the face by another his sister had just let go of. He shouted in surprise as she looked back and giggled.

"I thought you'd be happy to explore these woods. Weren't you the one who wanted to see if that old, abandoned manor was still around?" she teased.

"Great Aunt Belinda said they tore that shack down years ago. Besides, I don't think we would ever find it in this jungle!" Stephen started, but he stopped when Victoria held up her hand.

"Hold on; I think I see a small clearing ahead."

"Good; I need to catch my breath anyway."

The twins emerged in a small open area surrounded by old oak and elm trees on all sides. Stephen spotted an old stump and went to sit down, only to see a crack with a large spiderweb inside. Slightly recoiling in fear, he decided he would keep standing. Victoria went over to a huge oak tree and started to climb it. After a few minutes, she had gotten as far up as she dared.

"Do you see the way out from up there?" Stephen called out from below her.

"I still can't see anything. It's just too thick!" she replied with a little worry in her voice. She jumped to the ground and brushed some bits of bark off her jeans. "I don't think we're that lost. We've only been away for half an hour."

"You can cover a lot of ground in half an hour."

Victoria sighed and walked over to where they had entered the clearing. She knew her brother had been irritable ever since their parents had sent them to their great aunt's house instead of letting them stay home for the summer. To be honest, she wasn't too happy about it herself. They were sixteen and could look after themselves. But she was thankful for the time away from the city and that she had plenty of time to train for her next martial arts competition. As her mind wandered into thinking over her strategy for winning the next match her brother's voice broke her thoughts.

"Tori, can I ask you a question?"

"Fire away."

"Why did we leave our phones at the house again?"

"Because there's no signal out here, so they wouldn't be much use. We could barely get any at the house, and I was told by the old fellow at the diner that there certainly wouldn't be any here," she replied, knowing that it wasn't her best answer.

"Still seems kind of dumb to me," Stephen said as he pulled out his Swiss army knife and began to sharpen a stick he had found on the ground. He watched his sister looking around the edge of the clearing. He didn't want to admit it, but he was somewhat enjoying their little adventure, even though they were lost. He had already finished reading all the books he had brought with him, and when the gentleman at the diner told them about the abandoned manor, he wanted to investigate, despite how silly the whole thing sounded.

"Well, I can barely make out the trail from here; maybe we should have brought a machete or something? I cannot believe how overgrown the trails are," Victoria said, sounding even more worried than she was before.

"We could have brought our fencing foils."

"You only brought them so you could spar with me. They're too flimsy for much else, especially chopping through thick underbrush." Victoria paused while taking another look at the supposed path. "Let's keep going. I've got a good feeling about this trail," she said.

She and Stephen moved on through the woods, stopping every now and then to try and find their bearings. After another half an hour, moving through the dense forest, Stephen grabbed his sister by the shoulder and pointed to their right.

"Hey, Tori, wait just a second. There's something over there."

Victoria turned to where her brother was pointing and saw what had grabbed her brother's attention. It looked like the top half of a tube made of plants and vines that had been bent over and fastened together. It looked strange and out of place and yet somehow completely natural. She wondered what could have formed it when Stephen interrupted her thoughts.

"Let's go check it out. It might be a secret passage or something!" he said, now sounding a little excited.

They both hurried over to the tube and tried to peer inside, only to find it was too thick to look through.

Victoria looked closer and said, "It's probably a den of some sort. We should leave it alone. We don't want to disturb any wild animals."

Steve responded, "I doubt it. Look how it goes through the forest in both directions. It's almost like the outside of a tunnel."

Sure enough, the archway continued as far as she could see in both directions. "I'm going to climb it and see if I can find a way in," she said while moving closer.

"Be careful. It might be covering a trap or something," Stephen warned.

But she paid him no mind as she slowly began to climb up the arch. To her surprise, it held her weight, and she was able to make her way to the top. Once she was there, she tried to peer through the archway but was still unable to do so.

"I have an idea: I am going to try cutting a hole in it, so we can see inside," Stephen said as he pulled out his knife, opened its little hacksaw blade, and began to cut away at the side of the tunnel below Victoria.

"Wait! Let me get down first!" she shouted at her brother. She tried to climb down, but it was too late. The archway began to sag and then gave way beneath her, and she fell through the tunnel roof. Her feet landed on dirt, but she felt a sharp pain in the nape of her neck. Her long ponytail had caught in the branches that made up the tunnel roof, but thankfully, she wasn't hanging by it. "Steve! I told you to wait! Now, my hair is stuck in the roof!" she said in annoyance.

"Hang on, Tori. I'll get you free in no time," Stephen said with a laugh as he began to kick at the branches that formed the wall. Soon, he was able to smash his way into the tunnel. He couldn't help but laugh again at the sight of his sister's long black hair caught in the roof. He jumped up and managed to yank it free from the branches. He then stopped to look around at the tunnel. It was about six feet tall where Victoria's weight had caused the roof to sag and eventually fall through, but the rest was around seven feet tall, with the tunnel floor being around five feet wide. Despite their not being able to see into the tunnel from the outside, it was fairly well-lit from the sunlight shining through cracks in the walls and the holes he and Victoria had created. The light was a faint shade of green from the leaves and vines it was cascading through, and it gave the whole tunnel a strange look.

"I have never seen anything like this before," Victoria said in wonder as the twins kept looking around in amazement. "How do you think the sunlight can get through the walls? We could not see anything from the outside, but you would think that the walls had windows."

Stephen walked over to the hole he had made and poked his head out. "Tori, you are not going to believe this, but I think the bushes are somehow letting only the light through and yet keeping us from looking in," he said in bewilderment.

"That's completely impossible!" Victoria said in disbelief as she walked over to the other side of the tunnel and sat down on the soft earth. "This makes no sense at all!"

"So what are we going to do now?" Stephen asked as he walked over to his sister and put his hand on her shoulder. "Do you think we should climb out of here and try to find our way back to Great Aunt Belinda's? Or should we follow this tunnel and see where it leads?" He held out his hand to pull her up. Victoria grabbed it and stood up, brushing the dirt off her jeans and t-shirt.

"Well, we weren't making any progress plowing through the woods. I'd say we should try the tunnel, but which way should we go?" she asked as she looked in both directions.

Stephen rubbed his chin for a moment. "Let's head to the left," he said, pointing to the left of where they had entered. "If it turns out to be a dead end, we can always turn around anyway," he said as he walked away down the unnatural, yet somehow natural, tunnel. Victoria followed him as they made their way through it.

After a while of walking, with only the noise of the breeze rustling the leaves overhead to be heard, Stephen's voice broke the silence.

"Hey, Tori. I'm sorry for being rude to you back there and for making you fall through the roof. I just didn't think about what I was doing."

Victoria stopped. Stephen halted as well and turned to face her. She walked up to him and messed up his short black hair with her hands.

"I forgive you, Steve. I know you didn't really mean any harm," she said, laughing as he tried to fix his messed-up hair. "I know that both of us haven't been in the best mood ever since Mom and Dad dropped us off at Great Aunt Belinda's house. I'm still wondering why they couldn't just leave us at home. We are sixteen after all."

"I know; maybe they just wanted us to be away from the house for a bit. We've both been doing a lot of stuff, and we haven't been able to just sit back and relax for a while. Maybe this trip can be good for us if we let it," Stephen said quietly as they continued their walk through the wooden tunnel.

After another fifteen minutes of walking, they noticed the tunnel ahead getting brighter and that it was beginning to get larger. Suddenly, they turned a corner and found the tunnel opening into a large area of forest.

They stepped out into the sunlight that was now turning to dusk and examined their surroundings. The area was not unlike the forest that they had been wandering through, but all the underbrush had been cleared away, leaving only the large trees that still covered their view of the sky. But what surprised them the most was what was under and around the trees.

"Houses?" Stephen asked in shock.

"It's like an elf village in a fairytale book," Victoria said. She was in just as much shock as her brother. There were small houses made of wood dotted all over like a small city. There were paths of dry, bare earth connecting the homes, and they could see what seemed to be some shops and stalls towards the center of the city in what they guessed to be a marketplace. There were a few wagons and carts tied to some trees, and the market stalls were packed with all manner of produce, strange clothes, tools, and wooden crafts. The twins could even smell some food cooking in some of the houses as well.

However, there was one thing that worried them the most.

"If this is a village, then where are the people?" Victoria asked.

"Maybe they're all hiding from us," Stephen replied. He then called out: "We come in peace! We don't mean any harm!"

He was answered only by silence.

"Maybe we should look around," Victoria suggested. "We might find some clues to why nobody is here."

Stephen nodded, and they walked into the seemingly-abandoned town, looking into any doorways or windows as they passed. The whole place was giving off a very creepy feel, and both were getting a little unnerved.

Stephen walked around a corner and felt his foot hit something. He stopped and looked down, and what he saw made his blood run cold. There, at his feet, were some dolls all arranged in a circle, almost like a child's tea party, only there were no children to be seen.

"Hey, Tori...come look at this!" Stephen called out to his sister.

Tori hurried over and froze as soon as she saw the toys.

"That's not unsettling at all," she commented sarcastically.

Even through her tone, Stephen could tell that Victoria was as scared as he was. Stephen bent down, picked up one of the dolls, and looked at it before looking around them.

"It looks like whoever lives here just disappeared. Everything is still where it should be," he said as he dropped the doll on the ground.

"Do you think someone or something attacked them?" Victoria asked.

"No. There are no signs of a fight; nothing is broken; everything is laid out neatly. It's as if there was a busy village here and then everyone vanished into thin air."

"I'd say 'vanished' is a good word for it."

After a few more minutes of slowly walking through the quiet village, Stephen's voice broke the silence.

"M-maybe we should just head back," Stephen said, his voice quivering. "I'm really starting to get freaked out."

"Yeah, I'm with you there," Victoria said as they both turned back towards the tunnel entrance and began to walk back, only to stop when they heard the sound of two swords being drawn from their scabbards. They turned around to see two figures clad in gleaming armor and armed with swords, standing in the middle of the road to their right.

"Halt!" the knights shouted in unison as they charged towards the stunned twins, their swords raised and ready to strike.

"Where did they come from?!" Stephen shouted as he and Victoria started to run back the way they came from, only to see the tunnel entrance blocked by two more knights wielding large spears.

The twins knew they had only one option left: they had to fight.

Chapter 2. The Great Story.

"Surrender, intruders!" the sword-wielding knights both shouted as they moved closer to the twins, who in response, got into a fighting stance, ready to stand their ground.

The first knight swung his sword at Victoria, who spun around with a roundhouse kick, hitting the knight's wrist and knocking his sword out of his hand. Stephen dove for the falling sword and managed to grab its hilt and block the second attacker's swing. The first knight looked at Victoria in surprise but was quickly forced to move his arms up to defend against the flurry of attacks launched by the martial artist Victoria, who was now on the offensive. Stephen and the second knight were in an even sword fight, but with a fencer's agility and a quick twist of his wrist, Stephen had disarmed the knight, his opponent's sword flying into the dirt, with the tip sticking into the ground. Victoria ducked low, swept the first knight's legs out from under him, and he fell to the ground with a hard *thud*. Stephen held the point of the sword to the second knight's throat.

"Surrender," Stephen growled. He stared at the two knights, who looked at each other, and just as they appeared, they vanished into thin air.

"What?! How did they do that?" Victoria asked. She ran over to the second knight's sword that was still sticking out of the ground and pulled it out. The twins held their captured weapons in a ready stance as they stood back-to-back, waiting for another attack. They looked back at the tunnel entrance, only to see the two knights that were blocking their escape were also nowhere to be found.

"Do you think we scared them off?" Victoria asked, still panting from the fight.

"I doubt it. If they really can camouflage themselves like that, I bet they are just regrouping for another attack," Stephen responded breathlessly.

Then, just as Stephen had guessed, they were suddenly surrounded by a large force of knights, who had, again, appeared out of thin air, their swords drawn and spears lowered.

"Guards! Be ready to attack on my command!" shouted one of the knights in the group.

Stephen and Victoria braced themselves for the coming fight, but, just then, an older voice broke the tension.

"Stand down, men!" he called out, and the guards immediately sheathed their swords, raised their spears, and moved back, as the figure of an elderly person slowly walked towards the twins through the dense crowd.

The twins could not believe their eyes when they saw the figure. He was about their height and, for the most part, looked human. He had a long white beard and a balding head, wore a brown robe, and walked with an ornately-carved wooden staff. But his skin was a deep green; six fingers gripped his walking staff, and six toes stuck out of worn sandals under his robe. When he was closer to the twins, they could see that he had pointed ears on the sides of his head, and his eyes had thin catlike pupils that were bright yellowish-orange.

"I am sorry for the attack, young ones. We do not get many visitors in this part of the forest, let alone folks who look like you. I am Geltian, leader of this fine village of Tredut," the elder said in a smooth, warm tone.

"We didn't mean any harm. We had gotten lost in the woods behind our great aunt's house, found your tunnel, and followed it here," Victoria said as she lowered her sword and motioned for Stephen to do the same.

"You mean you have never been in this forest before?" Geltian asked.

"No. We wandered into the tunnel and found ourselves here. Then, your guards attacked us," Stephen explained.

"I see," the elder said, stroking his beard, deep in thought. He began to walk around the twins, looking them over and muttering to himself. As the elder continued to circle the twins, two of the guards walked up to them and removed their helmets, revealing their faces. They both had similar features to the elder, except one had light green skin, and the other was more of earthy-brown color.

"We are sorry for attacking you. It is just that we have not seen anyone like you before," the first guard said.

"Could we have our swords back?" the other asked sheepishly.

The twins held out their captured weapons, and the guards took them and put them back in their sheaths.

"That was an impressive move you made there. I would have never thought of kicking the sword out of my hand," the first guard commented before walking away.

"Could you teach me that trick you did with your wrist?" the second guard asked Stephen, but before he could answer, the elder held up his hands for silence and then turned to the twins again.

"What are your names?" he asked them.

"My name is Stephen, and this is my twin sister Victoria," Stephen answered.

"Did...did you say she is your twin?" the elder inquired with a quiver in his voice.

"Um, yes. We're twins. What about it?" Victoria asked.

The elder's face went from one of deep thought to pure joy. He raised his staff in the air and shouted: "Praise The One Above! Everyone! They are The Chosen Ones! The time has come! Quickly! We must prepare a feast in honor of this occasion!"

At this, the guards began cheering and tossing their helmets in the air, and the whole village came alive, with more and more citizens appearing in the houses, windows, doorways, and streets. The villagers looked just like the guards, only they were dressed as medieval civilians. The men wore long robes or tunics and trousers. The women were wearing mostly long dresses with flowing sleeves; a few ladies who were working on a rooftop were dressed in long tunics, vests, and loose trousers. As soon as the villagers appeared, they joined in the cheering, and a few children, dressed much like their adult counterparts, ran up to the twins and hugged them before running off again.

After a few minutes of excitement, the elder and an older woman, who wore a long grey and white dress, approached the twins.

"This is my wife Velien. Please come with us. We have a big celebration planned for tonight!" Geltian said as he and his wife gently ushered the twins into one of the little houses. It was a modest single-story house built against the back of a very large tree.

Once they were inside, the twins looked around at the cozy little home. It had a few rooms connected to the large sitting and dining room at the front of the house. There were a table and chairs in the middle of the room as well as a few padded benches in the corners. In the adjoining rooms, they could also see some beds and large wardrobes. All the furniture was made of wood and looked rustic but elegant with ornate carvings that decorated each piece.

"This is a very nice home, sir," Victoria commented.

"Thank you!" Geltian said. "I made the furniture myself, and my lovely Velien added the carvings. Now, please make yourselves comfortable. I am sure you have a lot of questions to ask, and I will do my best to answer them all."

They all sat down around the table, and Velien left the room, only to return in a few moments with a tray with wooden cups filled with tea.

"Before I ask the big question, I really would like to know how you are able to vanish into thin air so quickly," Victoria said.

"Well, that is an easy question to answer. You see, we Kittrian are able to change the color of our skin to better blend into our surroundings," Velien replied.

"But your clothes too?" Victoria countered.

"As long as the clothes are made of a natural material, we can change their colors, too, if we focus hard enough. Some of us are quite good at it, while others are not," Geltian explained. "And if you are wondering about the guards' armor and weapons, they are actually made of the bark of a special kind of tree we grow in a grove to the north. The bark is nearly as strong as metal but half the weight, and when you polish it, it turns a bright shade of grey, so one really cannot tell the difference between it and metal just by looking at it."

"That is really interesting. But now for the big question: what is this whole 'chosen one' deal you're saying we are?" Stephen asked before taking a drink from his cup.

The elder leaned back in his chair and sighed. "Long ago, well before my time, there was a war between the peoples of this land we call Lulandal. The mighty tribe known as the Unkarians had taken control of the underground tribes and creatures and rose up to try and conquer the whole land. They were eventually defeated, and the Unkarians were all but wiped out, with one of the remaining leaders vowing that one day, they would return and defeat us.

"After the war was over, the other tribes gathered in a great conference and discussed what they should do to prepare for the future. Some said that they should go back to the Black Peak and kill all the remaining Unkarians and their kin to prevent such a war from happening again. Others said to leave them alone and that they could never take over the whole land again with their reduced numbers. Both sides became angry at the other's ideas and were nearly at a breaking point, when a wise old Kittrian walked into the middle of the room between the arguing factions. He then told what is now known as the Great Story: a story of three people, two of whom were twins from another world, banding together to end the Unkarian threat for good. The elder then collapsed and died after finishing his story, leaving the whole assembly in stunned silence.

"Since then, the Great Story has been passed down through the generations in all the tribes, and we have been awaiting the day for the three heroes to come. And once we received word that the Chosen hero from our world had been identified, we knew it was only a matter of time before the twins appeared."

"And I assume that means us?" Victoria asked.

"Yes, young one," Velien said with a big smile. "We have been waiting for you for so long. I cannot tell you just how happy I am to see the Great Story coming true!"

"Now, we must get you ready for the feast tonight!" Geltian said, standing from his chair.

"What do you mean?" Stephen asked as he and his sister also stood.

"Well, the attire from your world does not lend itself very well for a proper Kittrian feast," Velien said, gesturing to the twins' jeans, t-shirts, and hiking boots. "We must make sure you look presentable for the people tonight!"

At that, Velien gently took Victoria's hand, led her into one of the side rooms, and closed the door behind them, while Geltian took Stephen into a different room. He then went over to an ornate wooden wardrobe and brought out an array of tunics, robes, and trousers, all in various colors.

"I think some of these should fit you well enough. I will let you figure out what suits you best," Geltian said as he left the room.

AFTER SETTLING ON A forest green tunic with gold leaves embroidered into it, matching trousers, a brown vest, a leather belt with some pouches attached to it, and some very comfortable leather boots, Stephen had finished getting dressed and was sitting on the bed when heard a knock at the door.

"Are you decent?" he heard his sister ask from the other side of the door. "Velien said we need to come out as soon as it gets dark. That's when the feast can begin."

"Yeah, I just finished. Come on in," he answered as he bent down to adjust his left boot. He heard Victoria open the door and quickly close it behind her.

"You look like Robin Hood," she said with a chuckle.

Stephen looked up, and he felt his jaw hit the floor when he saw his sister. Her slender five-foot-seven form was adorned with a flowing emerald dress with long, wide sleeves. Her long black hair had been braided into a single plait down her back with various wildflowers twisted into it. He'd seen her dressed up for church or the occasional wedding, but this was on a whole other level.

"You look like a princess or a really fancy elf," Stephen said.

"Thanks," Victoria replied rather sheepishly. "I feel kind of silly in this. I mean, I don't mind dressing up, but this is way more than I am used to. Velien kept insisting I wear all this," she said, giving the dress a little twirl and then with a sigh, she added, "Too bad I probably can't take this to prom in a year or two. I'd be the talk of the whole school!"

"Maybe you could ask Velien if you could have it," Stephen offered with a laugh.

Victoria chuckled uneasily and shook her head, her face showing a worried expression as she walked over to the bed and sat down next to Stephen.

"Steve, do you think what they're saying is true? That we and another person are supposed to save the whole land from some evil tribe?" Victoria asked with a nervous tone.

"Maybe. I think it sounds rather exciting," Stephen said. "I mean, look at it this way: do you remember reading all those fantasy books when we were kids? I remember how we used to pretend to travel to those mystical worlds and have all kinds of adventures. And now it looks like we are actually in a real fantasy world! How cool is that? And to top it all off, who is better qualified for the job than us?"

Victoria looked at him in annoyance and kicked his right leg with her leather boot. "I know we have a lot of useful skills that would come in handy if we do decide to 'fulfill the Great Story,' but doesn't it seem like a lot of work for two sixteen-year-olds?" Victoria asked, now with worry fully evident in her voice.

Stephen slid closer to her and put his arm around her shoulder. "Listen, Tori. I know this is a lot to take in. I'm not sure of it myself to be honest. But what I do know is this: we were brought into this world for a purpose, and if there are people out there who do indeed need our help, I intend to help them. Besides, between our sword-fighting know-how, my tactical knowledge, and your martial arts skills, we shouldn't have much of a problem dealing with a small tribe of bad guys," Stephen said as he and Victoria stood up together and hugged. "I know that together we can do it," he added reassuringly.

"T-thanks, Steve," Victoria said, still with a quiver in her voice. "I am excited to see what this world has to offer. Like you said, I remember when we were younger, playing pretend in the woods with our friends and wishing we were in the fantasy books we were reading, but now that we may indeed be in a fantasy story...it's not what I imagined at all. Already, we have had to fight for our lives against those guards. I know they didn't know who we were at the time, but just the thought of us having to fight off some big bad guy is a little daunting."

"You're right, Tori. I won't deny it is a little unnerving, but I still think we could do some good here. Besides, what's a little adventure without some danger, right?" Stephen asked. "Now, they said something about a big feast, didn't they? I hope we didn't get all dressed up for nothing! Come on! Let's go enjoy what they call 'a proper Kittrian feast!'" Stephen said as they left the room together.

As they reached the door leading out of the house, they could see through the windows that it was getting dark outside and, to both of their surprise, they saw not one, not two, but three small moons lighting up the night sky through the trees above them. The furthest one on the right was a pale white and rather large; the middle was almost a light blue, the smallest of the three and lower than the first, while the third was higher than the others and more of an orange-ish color.

Victoria grabbed Stephen's arm in fear, as they saw the proof that they were indeed no longer in their world. They then took a deep breath and, together, they opened the door.

Chapter 3. The Journey Begins.

When the twins stepped outside, they were greeted by Geltian and Velien standing about fifteen feet away, facing them. Between them and the twins were six guards holding long spears, three on each side facing each other, their armor gleaming in the moonlight.

"Now that our honored guests have arrived, the Feast of The Chosen One can begin!" Geltian shouted.

The guards raised their spears and then hit the end of each spear on the ground in unison three times. On the third strike, the whole area was lit up by hundreds of colorful lamps that were hung from the trees. The lamps revealed dozens of tables and benches all decorated with many kinds of fruits, vegetables, meats, drinks, and desserts. The twins could see a group of musicians on one side, with several kinds of instruments, and the rest of the villagers, who were dressed in bright festive attire, standing around them.

Once the people saw the twins, the silence was destroyed by the cheer that erupted from the crowd. The twins were soon escorted to the seats of honor next to Geltian and his wife as well as several other village leaders. There was no shortage of food, drinks, music, and dancing for the rest of the night. And despite their apprehension, the twins began to genuinely enjoy themselves at the feast as they were treated like royalty by all in attendance.

After everyone had finally had their fill and were too tired to even sway to the music, they all began to quietly go back to their homes. The twins were gently led back to Geltian's house and shown to their rooms. Stephen fell asleep almost immediately, but Victoria stayed awake a while longer, looking out of the window at the three moons, wondering what she and her brother had gotten themselves into. She closed the window shutters, threw herself onto the bed, and silently hoped that everything would be alright during their adventure in this new world. She soon fell asleep and did not wake up until the sunlight was coming through the cracks in the shutters.

WHEN VICTORIA GOT UP, she found that Velien had left a blue tunic, a brown leather belt and vest, brown trousers, and large leather walking boots for her. Once she was dressed, she walked into the main room, and she noticed a plate with what looked to be a buttered biscuit, some pieces of yellow meat that looked and smelled like bacon, and some bluish eggs that were somehow still steaming, waiting for her on the table.

She ate her fill and then went outside and saw the village was bustling with activity, with people working and children playing. She then heard the familiar metal-on-metal clash of a sword fight, and she quickly hurried over to investigate. She soon saw what was making the noise: Stephen was sparring with the guard he had fought the day before. A small crowd had gathered to watch one of their guards duel one of their new heroes.

"Good! Now, just swing your sword, just like I showed you!" Stephen shouted as the guard attempted to copy Stephen's disarming maneuver that he had fallen for the day before. The guard twisted his sword around, and Stephen's weapon flew out of his hand and into the dirt.

The crowd of villagers applauded and began to disperse. Some children ran past Stephen and gave him a high five. Victoria smirked, knowing he must have taught them that.

"Great job! I told you that you could do it!" Stephen said as he retrieved his sword, walked forward, and shook the guard's hand before giving the sword back to him. The guard spotted Victoria and waved at her as he walked away.

"So you're training the locals now?" Victoria asked, returning the guard's wave.

"Good morning to you too," Stephen said jokingly. "When I got outside, he was waiting for me to show him how I managed to disarm him so easily yesterday. I must say he is a fast learner. That was only his second try, and he did it perfectly."

The twins started to walk back to Geltian's house, when another guard approached them.

"Stephen and Victoria, I have been sent to bring you to the meeting house right away. Geltian wishes to speak to you."

"Lead the way, then," Stephen replied as they followed the guard to a large building near the center of the village.

Once they walked through the double doors, they saw a large room with many wooden chairs and tables. In the center of the room, they saw Geltian standing over a large map on a table with a pile of scrolls and books nearby. Geltian looked up from the table and smiled at the twins.

"Thank you, Herett, you may go back to your duties," Geltian said.

The guard gave a quick bow and left the building.

Geltian then beckoned the twins over to the table and gestured to the map. "It is time you see more of our world. You are here in the village of Tredut." He gestured to a marking on the western edge of the map. He then pointed at a marking towards the center of the map. "The Chosen One is currently over here in Areiop. It is on the northeastern edge of the Highland Forest. It is a good day's journey from here, so I suggest you hurry, so you can meet up with him. We have already sent messages to the next village along the trail so that they will be expecting you."

"Will we be walking the whole way?" Victoria asked.

"I am afraid so. We do not have anything you could ride, other than a few of our farm animals," Geltian replied.

"That's alright. We're used to walking long distances back where we're from anyway," Stephen responded. "Besides, the path we came through was much too low for anyone riding an animal."

"Well, while that is true, the path to the north that connects our village to Fruniet and Areiop is actually higher, as we have Trodontian traders come by from time to time, and they are too tall for the southern paths. So we made sure to grow the northern paths differently to make them accessible," Geltian replied.

"Trodontians? Are they another tribe?" Victoria asked.

"That and another race altogether. I am certain you'll meet some eventually. Do not worry. They are normally a quite friendly folk; just remember to never pull their tails," Geltian said with a chuckle. "I did that once when I was a young lad, and I was only trying to be funny. I still have the scar on my back I received from that little stunt. Now, we need to make sure you have all you need for your journey. Velien is gathering some food and other supplies for you, while I am to take you to the smithy, so you can get something to protect yourselves along the path in case you have any trouble."

At this, Stephen's face lit up but then he noticed Victoria's look of concern.

"Will we be in any danger on the way to meet 'The Chosen One?'" Victoria asked, sounding worried.

"Not during the daytime, and even at night, the danger is quite minimal on the path. However, there is a significant clearing between the North and South Forests, where the Green River flows through towards the city of Areiop. Gritter raiding parties sometimes lurk around that area, but they are normally small in number, and gritters themselves are diminutive in stature and easily dealt with. I am quite sure two strong young warriors with fighting skills like yourselves will have no trouble dealing with a few gritters," Geltian said confidently.

With that, Geltian gave the twins a small copy of the map and led them out of the building and back into the town, which was still bustling with activity. He led them down a few dirt roads until they came to a stone building towards the outside of the village.

"This is the finest blacksmith we have in our village. He will give you the weapons that will aid your journey," Geltian said as he brought them inside.

The smithy was like most blacksmith shops the twins had seen pictures of in books and at various historical reenactments. There were several workbenches and shelves filled with various parts and tools. A small forge was in the corner, and its heat could be felt as soon as they stepped inside. On the walls hung many farming tools and, to Stephen's delight, weapons of all shapes and sizes. The blacksmith was bent over an anvil, hammering away on what looked to be a sickle.

"Hello there, Barit!" Geltian called out. "I have brought two fine young warriors who require weapons for their journey to Areiop!"

The blacksmith stood up and turned to face them. He was dressed in a soot-covered tunic, trousers, and a singed black apron. His long brown beard was singed and burned in a few places, and there were bits of still glowing metal entangled in it, but it couldn't hide his grin when he saw them.

"Ah! I have been waiting for you two!" he said excitedly. "I heard about how you two trounced the guards when you first arrived, and as soon as I heard that, I knew you would be the ones to help The Chosen One. Now, which one of you two knows how to wield a sword like a true soldier?"

"We both do, sir," Stephen replied. "We have been taking lessons for a few years now."

"You're still much better than me though," Victoria said, trying to be honest.

"Well, I have just the thing for you both," the smith said with a smile. He went over to one of the shelves, picked up a large wooden box, and brought it over to a workbench near the twins. "Go ahead and open it. Tell me what you think of them."

Stephen hurried over and opened the lid of the wooden box. He couldn't help but let out a little gasp in surprise at what he found. Two glimmering one-handed swords lay within. He quickly picked one up and looked it over. The blade was as straight as a measuring stick, and there wasn't an imperfection in the metal to be seen. The hilt and cross-guard were designed to look like vines intertwined with each other, with a golden oak leaf in the center of the cross-guard. Stephen couldn't help but wave it around a bit, finding that the sword was the perfect weight for him. Victoria picked up the other sword and saw that while it was nearly identical to her brother's, hers had a sparkling blue gem in the shape of a flower in the center of the cross-guard.

"It's perfect!" Stephen said, barely holding in his excitement, continuing to gaze at the sword and looking at his reflection in the blade.

"It's beautiful! Thank you, sir," Victoria added.

"Anything for The Chosen Ones," the blacksmith replied, still smiling. He then pulled out two sheaths and belts. "These are for the swords also. May they keep you safe on your travels."

"Thank you, Barit! As usual, your craftsmanship is unmatched!" Geltian said as he and the twins began to leave the smithy.

"Wait a moment!" the blacksmith called out after them. "I have one more gift for the young lady there." He brought down another large wooden box and beckoned for Victoria to open it. Victoria did and found two gauntlets and a pair of boots. They were made of leather and had plates of metal like the guard's armor fastened to them. "I was told you could fight with your hands and feet as well as a sword. These should be of some use to you. Go ahead and try them on."

Victoria did and found that not only did they fit perfectly, but they didn't weigh much more than her normal sparring gloves and hiking boots. They were also quite comfortable too.

"Thank you very much, sir. I can promise you I will put these to good use," she said with a smile.

"You are welcome, young one," the blacksmith said. "Now, go and save Lulandal!"

The twins thanked the blacksmith once again and quickly fastened their swords and sheaths to their belts before leaving the smithy.

As they walked through the town, they noticed that when they passed the villagers, they would stop what they were doing and begin to follow them. As they made their way to the northern edge of the village, they were met by Velien, who had brought them two packs with provisions for their journey, as well as extra clothes for the trip. Stephen looked over the map with Geltian, while Victoria put her extra-normal walking boots and the gauntlets into her pack. Soon, they were ready to start.

"You should reach Fruniet by late afternoon if you keep a good pace," Geltian said. "You could try to reach Areiop today, but it would be rather late at night. I would suggest you stay the night at Fruniet and continue your journey in the morning. I have already sent word to the elder of Fruniet, and he will be more than willing to accommodate you tonight."

"Anything we should know about the path ahead?" Stephen asked.

"Well, about a mile up the path is a bridge we grew over the Green River. The path then follows it until you get to Fruniet. From there, you follow the path until it opens in the clearing between the two major forests. You will cross the Green River again while in the clearing, and soon, you will find yourselves in Areiop," Velien answered. "It is a truly beautiful journey. Geltian and I have walked it many times."

"I'm looking forward to it," Stephen said confidently.

"On behalf of our humble village, I would like to wish you a good trip. May you be successful on this mission!" Geltian said in a loud voice.

"Thank you so much for your hospitality!" Victoria said, hugging Velien.

"We are just so glad to be the first village you came to!" Velien said, hugging Victoria back. "Good luck! And may The One Above keep you safe."

The twins put the packs on their backs and began to walk towards the entrance of the path. When they entered it, they turned around and looked back at the villagers, who were still gathered around the entrance. When the villagers saw them turn back, they let out a deafening cheer and tossed their hats into the air. The twins smiled and waved back as they disappeared into the covered path.

The path was nearly identical to the first one the twins had encountered, but as Geltian said, it was nearly ten feet tall and eight feet wide. Apart from the gentle breeze coming through it, the tunnel was completely silent.

Suddenly, the silence was broken by the sound of a sword being drawn from its sheath. Victoria spun around, her hand on the hilt of her sword, only to see that Stephen was admiring his sword again. She sighed and kept walking. She could hear him swing the sword from time to time, occasionally hitting branches at the edge of the trail and cutting through them with ease.

After a while, they heard the sound of running water and knew they must be near the Green River. They picked up their pace and soon found the bridge Velien had mentioned. It was made from vines and trees grown together like the tunnel walls. It also had a roof and even some branches that stuck out like benches along the sides. There, the twins stopped for a lunch break, eating some of the dried fruits and meat Velien had placed in their packs.

After resting for half an hour, the twins got up and continued their trek northward. Their trek was uneventful, and, after a few hours, they found themselves nearing another village late in the afternoon.

There was a small group of guards waiting for them at the entrance, and when they saw them approaching, they stood at attention and told them that the elder was waiting for them at the large building at the center of the village. The twins followed the guards' instructions and went into the center of the town. As they passed the townsfolk, they noticed some people would stop and stare for a moment before turning back to their work; others would ignore them altogether.

"I guess we're not big celebrities here," Stephen said. "After what the last village did, you'd think they would be over the moon that we arrived."

As they kept walking, some children playing a game ran past them. As they passed, one of the little girls, wearing a bright blue dress, ran close to Victoria, grabbed her by the arm, and tugged at it. Victoria looked down at the girl in surprise and saw she had a very worried look on her face.

"Do not stay here. You are not safe," she said before letting go of Victoria's arm and running off again, her long braids of white hair bobbing along behind her.

The girl was already out of sight before the twins could even respond. They looked at each other and moved on.

Soon, the twins came to the large meeting hall, and they saw a very nicely dressed younger man standing by the doors, looking nervously around him and wringing his hands.

"Hello, there!" Stephen called out to him. "Are you the elder of this village?"

Hearing the greeting, the man turned to face the twins, and his expression turned from one of worry to one of nervous relief.

"You...you are actually here!" he said excitedly. "Please come inside immediately! I have dinner waiting for you."

The twins followed him inside and found that a decently-sized meal was indeed waiting for them. The man introduced himself as the elder and explained over dinner that he was the son of an elder who had passed away recently, and he was made the elder in his place. During the rest of the meal, he continued to talk about various things, from the weather and the history of the village to questions about the twins and where they came from.

After dinner, the elder told them about his plans for them that evening.

"So I have a house cleared and ready for you to stay in for the night. I will take you there myself after I introduce you to the townsfolk and tell them how we are going to be helping you with your important mission. Then, tomorrow morning, I will make sure you are properly trained by the best swordsman in my village. And after that, I have some important people I want you to meet," he said matter-of-factly.

Victoria and Stephen looked at each other and frowned. They didn't have to say anything to each other, as both of them knew something was up.

"Actually, we were planning on continuing our trip tonight. Geltian said that Areiop isn't too far away from here, and we could reach it in a few more hours," Stephen said.

"What?! That old fool does not know what he is talking about!" the elder shouted, jumping up from his chair in a rage. "There is little chance you will make it there before daybreak, if you can make it there at all!"

The twins stood up from their places with their hands on the hilts of their swords.

"We appreciate the meal, but we really must be going now," Victoria said, grabbing Stephen by the arm and pulling him towards the door. The elder started to protest, but when he saw Stephen beginning to unsheathe his sword, he backed off.

The twins grabbed their packs and began to hurry to the tunnel entrance. As they were nearly out of the village, the elder came running over.

"You know there was a raiding party of gritters spotted in the clearing, correct? It would not be wise to travel after dark!" he shouted, his face barely holding back a sinister smile.

Stephen and Victoria responded by drawing their swords. "I think we can handle a few critters ourselves. Thank you for the warning, though!" Stephen shouted sarcastically.

The twins hurried away from the village, and once they were back on the path leading to Areiop and out of sight of the village, they stopped to catch their breath.

"What was all that about?" Victoria asked.

"I think that elder was a traitor."

"And what makes you say that?" Victoria asked sarcastically.

"Easy. He slipped up twice: first, when he got mad at us for trying to leave, and second, when he mentioned that there was a raiding party nearby. What if he was going to try and keep us overnight, only to let us get 'kidnapped' after dark?"

"Then that little girl's warning makes sense. She must have known what was going on. I hope she doesn't get into trouble on account of us not playing along."

The twins sheathed their swords, and just as they were about to start walking again Victoria felt a tug on her arm. She turned around, only to see a small figure in a green cloak standing beside her. Its hood obscured most of the figure's face besides two long braids of white hair going down their front. Victoria jumped back in surprise and accidentally knocked the figure down. When the figure hit the ground, their hood fell back to reveal the little girl they had met in the village.

"I'm so sorry! I didn't mean to knock you down," Victoria said as she leaned down and helped the little girl on her feet.

"I guess I deserve that for scaring you," the girl said as she dusted herself off.

"It's alright. I'm just not used to people appearing out of nowhere," Victoria replied.

"I remember you from earlier. What's your name?" Stephen asked.

"My name is Annalio. My friends call me Annie," she said.

"Well, Annie, my name is Victoria, but you can call me Tori, and this is my brother Stephen. You can call him Steve if you want. I'd say you can consider us friends after giving us that warning earlier," Victoria told Annie.

"I did not want you to be captured. I saw the elder meeting with an evil creature last night, and I knew he was up to something and that I had to warn you somehow when you came here," Annie replied.

"I hope this won't get you into too much trouble," Stephen said. He was concerned about their new little friend's safety.

"Oh, no. Nobody saw me leave, so I should be fine. That is the benefit of being able to turn invisible; even my own brother cannot see me when I do not want him to. Not many Kittrians are able to completely disappear at my age," Annie said with a wry smile.

"Good. Now, you'd better go home before someone thinks you're missing and gets suspicious," Victoria said as she knelt and hugged Annie.

"I will. Goodbye, Tori...Steve. I hope you get to Areiop safely. May The One Above see you safely there," Annie said as she pulled her hood up and vanished again. But even though the twins couldn't see her, they heard her voice come out of thin air: "One more thing: once you leave the forest and find the Green River, follow it south for about a mile. There is an old bridge you can try and cross there. I heard the elder tell the bad creatures to wait for you on the other side of the new bridge in case you tried to get to Areiop tonight. I will try to send a message to Areiop, so they can send some help."

"Thank you, Annie," Victoria whispered. She then turned to Stephen and said, "I hope she'll be alright."

"I think she will be. She seems like a clever girl," Stephen replied.

The twins then began to walk on in silence again. By the time the sun had gone down, they had reached the end of the tunnel, crossed a bridge over the Green river, and they could see the clearing ahead of them. The dirt road stretched onwards across the glade, cutting through the tall grass like a knife, and the twins could see the river a few miles away, glimmering in the moonlight.

"Well, there's the river Annie described. I can't believe how bright it is out here," Victoria remarked.

"It must be the three moons," Stephen said. "But if we can see, that means other things can see us too. We should stay low and stay quiet."

Victoria silently nodded, and the twins began to quietly creep across the glade.

As they approached the river, they saw the bridge across it only a few hundred yards away and small fires on the other side of the river. They could see the tree line and the tunnel opening just a short distance away from the small fires. The twins crouched down in some bushes near the road.

"That must be the raiding party the elder mentioned. I'll bet they're just waiting for us to fall right into their trap," Stephen whispered.

"Let's do what Annie suggested and head south along the riverbank. There's plenty of bushes we can hide in," Victoria whispered back as she pulled the gauntlets the blacksmith had given her out of her pack and slipped them on. "We should be ready for a fight in case some of the raiders are on our side of the river."

The twins silently moved down the riverbank and soon saw the old bridge Annie had mentioned. It was an old stone bridge that was crumbling away in some places but seemed intact for the most part.

"I'll go first," Victoria suggested as she gingerly stepped onto the old stone structure. Stephen followed her onto the bridge as they carefully crossed the river, stepping over some parts that had completely fallen away. Just as they neared the other side, they saw, to their dismay, that the pathway had crumbled, leaving a gap nearly five feet wide.

Stephen mouthed that he would jump first and took a running leap. He made it across and held out his arms for Victoria to grab onto when she jumped. Victoria stepped back a few paces, took a running start, jumped, and barely landed on the edge. She lost her balance and let out a quick gasp of fear as she began to fall towards the water below. Stephen lunged forward and barely managed to grab her by her sword belt and pull her back onto the bridge.

"Thanks for the catch. Do you think they heard me?" Victoria asked breathlessly.

"Maybe. We should hurry before they come looking for us," Stephen said as they hurried across the bridge and into the brush on the riverbank, crouching down as soon as they entered the grass.

They slowly crept through the tall grass and towards the forest. Suddenly, they could hear rustling in the underbrush and what sounded like strange squeaks and grunts. The twins had their swords out in seconds as they spotted several dark figures with glowing red eyes emerging from the grass. They were barely three feet high, with dark, stone-like skin, large ears the stuck out from their heads, and large hands and feet with razor-sharp claws. Within moments, the twins were surrounded where they stood, back-to-back, their swords drawn.

"These must be the gritters Geltian talked about," Victoria said.

"They don't look like much! We can take them!" Stephen shouted.

One of the gritters screeched and charged, with the rest of them following.

The lead gritter jumped for Victoria, but she was already swinging her sword, which met the gritter's neck and severed its head from its body, which fell lifeless at her feet. Stephen swung his sword in a wide arc, killing four gritters at once. Another gritter came at Victoria as she was slicing a gritter to her right, and she sent it flying into the river with a kick. Stephen bent low and started sweeping his sword back and forth in front of him, clearing a path through the gritters as more and more of them came pouring out of the grass.

"Follow me! I'll clear a path to the woods! Just keep them off my back!" Stephen shouted as he marched forward, cutting down gritters by the dozen.

Victoria stayed right behind her brother, slicing, kicking, and punching any gritters that came too close.

"They aren't that tough after all!" She cried over the gritters' screeches and growls.

"Let's see you say that when we're completely swarmed! There's just no end to them!" Stephen yelled.

Just then, a shadow fell on them from above as something large blocked some of the moonlight. The twins and the gritters stopped their fighting for a moment and looked up to see what had created the shadow.

Then, a deafening hawk-like screech was heard before a loud voice boomed.

"Tally Ho!"

Before Victoria had a chance to react, a large bird-like creature swooped down and grabbed her by her shoulders, lifting her into the air. She screamed as she disappeared into the sky above the trees.

"Tori!" Stephen shouted, breaking into a sprint, smashing his way through the remaining gritters.

As he kept running, he could hear hoofbeats thundering towards him from behind. He turned around, only to see the arm of a person on horseback grab him by the front of his tunic and swing him onto the horse's back behind them.

"Hold on! I will get you to safety!" A feminine voice shouted.

Stephen grabbed onto the rider's back. He could feel the gritters getting knocked aside by the horse as they thundered towards the opening in the forest path. But just before they made it, Stephen heard a roar come from behind him and felt a large object hit him in the back of his head, and everything went black.

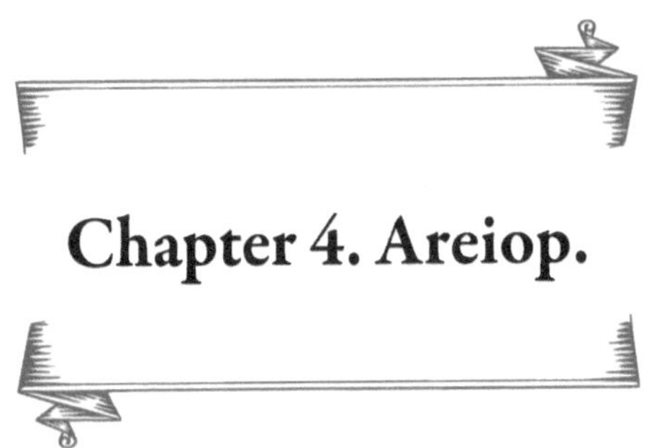

Chapter 4. Areiop.

"Tori!" Stephen shouted as he woke up in a comfortable bed.

He sat bolt-upright and looked around the room he found himself in. It was not unlike his little room in Geltian's house; the furniture was all made of wood and had ornate carvings decorating each piece. He jumped up out of the bed only to crumble into a heap when he landed on his right foot. He winced in pain as he pulled up his trouser leg to see a bandage covering a large gash in his leg, where he must have been injured in the fight the previous night. He then felt a rush of pain from his left arm and head. He gingerly reached out a hand and felt those places, finding some more bandages.

"I don't remember any of those things even getting close enough to scratch me last night," he mused to himself as he slowly walked to the door leading out of his room and opened it. As soon as he began to turn the knob, the door flew open, and he was engulfed in a hug by his sister.

"Steve! I'm so glad you're okay!" she said excitedly.

Stephen yelped in pain and pushed Victoria away.

"Sorry, Steve. I forgot you were injured. Those things really did a number on you."

"I'm alright. I'm just glad to see you're okay. I admit I panicked when that...that *thing* carried you off. I must have let my guard down when I started chasing you; some of those gritters must have gotten some cheap shots in while I was distracted, and I didn't even notice."

"Falamore said he couldn't carry us both, and he figured you could last a few seconds more until Windmere arrived."

"Falamore and Windmere?"

"Falamore is the Blakmian mercenary who grabbed me last night. They're a bird-like species and mostly live in the south. As for Windmere, I don't know any more than that she is a Trodontian, and she was the one who picked you up last night before a greature got a lucky shot in with a log and knocked you out," Victoria explained as she led him to a table and pulled out a chair for him to sit on.

"Okay, then. So where are we?" Stephen asked as he sat down, and Victoria grabbed some of the biscuits and gravy that were left out on the table.

"We're in Areiop. We made it after all," Victoria said with a smile. "Annie's message came through shortly after nightfall, and the city's elder sent the two mercenaries after us to make sure we arrived safely."

"That was nice of them. So if we are in Areiop, where is 'The Chosen One?'" He asked, his mouth full of biscuits and gravy.

"Technically, you've already met him. He was the one who bandaged you up when you arrived. I wasn't there right away, as the elder wanted me to tell him what had happened and where the raiding party was. I got here just as Groman was finishing bandaging you up. He's an excellent doctor. And I will say your constant asking for me in your delusion was very sweet," Victoria said with a grin as she watched her brother's face turn red.

"You've met him, then? How does he seem to you? Do you think he can fight?" Stephen asked, trying to get over his embarrassment.

"I'll let you find out yourself. I'm supposed to take you to Falamore and Groman once you're finished; they're waiting for you outside," Victoria said, helping Stephen to his feet.

The twins then walked to the door and strode out into the sunshine of the late morning.

Areiop was no different from the other Kittrian villages the twins had seen, other than that it seemed much larger, with more people wandering around, going about their daily business.

Stephen noticed a tall and muscular Kittrian man standing nearby who approached the twins when he saw them. He was slightly taller than the twins and dressed in normal Kittrian garb, but he had a large sword that was in a sheath attached to a belt on his back.

"It is good to see you on your feet, Stephen," the man said in a smooth voice. "I used the strongest of my herbs to take care of your injuries. Are you feeling better?"

"They are, actually. Thank you. Although I don't remember getting most of them besides getting hit in the head with that log," Stephen replied.

"Well, you must have been wounded just before Windmere picked you up, and after, she slowed her pace to make sure you did not fall off when you were knocked out. One of the gritters managed to jump on her back and slash you a few more times before she managed to throw it off," Groman said.

Stephen looked at him in shock. He could hardly believe all that had happened, and he didn't have any memory of it.

"Groman, where is Falamore?" Victoria asked.

"Oh, he was just scouting back where the greatures and gritters were hidden to make sure there were not any left to cause trouble," Groman answered. "He should return any minute now."

Just then, a loud voice was heard from above the group.

"Ho, there! I see the young swordsman is awake!" he shouted.

Groman looked up to the sky and cupped his hands around his mouth and cried, "He certainly is! He wants to meet you!"

Just then, a large, winged figure swooped down and landed near Groman; Stephen could hardly believe his eyes. The man was slightly shorter than himself but sported a massive pair of golden-brown feathered wings sprouting from his back and a similar tail behind him. His hands and feet were shaped like an eagle's and were covered in scaly skin, his fingers and toes were tipped with sharp talons, and the rest of his body besides his face was covered in feathers that matched his wings. His face, especially his nose, seemed pointed as if he had a beak like a bird, and his eyes were a brilliant shade of blue that seemed to pierce through anything or anyone he looked at. He was dressed in a sky-blue tunic and breeches that ended at his bird-like knees, which bent backward. He was armed with a longbow and a quiver full of arrows that were strapped to his back and, strangely enough, another longbow on his right leg and another quiver on his left leg, as well as two short swords in their scabbards at his sides.

The birdman stepped forward towards Stephen.

"Greetings, young lad. I am Falamore, sky warrior for hire, at your service," Falamore said with a bow.

"It is very nice to meet you, sir," Stephen said, "although I am a little upset about your carrying my sister off like that last night. You could have warned us you were coming."

"Lad, if I had given you and your sister warning, I would have given it to the enemy as well," Falamore said in a calm voice. "The 'Tally Ho!' was the best I could do before I was upon you and the lass."

"And you chose her instead of me...why?" Stephen questioned.

"The lass was smaller than you, and you were cutting your way through the gritters quite efficiently. I knew Windmere was nearing you at a fast pace and would arrive within a minute," Falamore replied. "Do you have any more questions?"

"Just one," Stephen said. "Are all those gritters gone? I want a rematch!"

Groman shook his head, Victoria groaned, and Falamore began to laugh heartily.

"Nay, lad! They have all run away! But I can say that because of you and the lass, some thirty gritters met their ends last night, and I daresay that is a good night's work," Falamore said with a smile. "But if fighting is your wish, you may swing your sword in battle yet again, lad. I sense that this is only the beginning of something much larger than we four can handle."

"Four? Aren't you forgetting someone? There's four of us already here," Victoria said.

"Did I?" Falamore asked jokingly with a chuckle. "Well, we shall find her at the smithy. I know that you young warriors have yet to meet a Trodontian; I say it is high time you do."

With that, the group started walking towards the eastern side of the city. As they walked, Stephen could feel the pain of his injuries begin to fade away.

"Groman, what did you put on my wounds?" Stephen asked as they walked.

"Just the freshest healing herbs I had on hand. Why? Are your wounds hurting again?" Groman inquired in a concerned tone.

"Just the opposite. They are feeling better by the minute. It's very impressive," Stephen replied.

"Oh, thank you. I have taken many lessons from the village healer, and I do enjoy being able to put my training to use," Groman said with a smile.

As they walked, Stephen and Victoria could hear someone banging on an anvil in the blacksmith shop.

"Ah, that would be Windmere," Falamore said. "She is never too far from a smithy, be it hers or someone else's."

They came around a corner, and there, they saw the blacksmith shop. It was designed similar to the other smithy the twins had received their swords in, but this one was larger and had an outdoor working area that had a roof and a five-foot-tall wooden wall at the bottom on the side that was facing them. There was open air between the wall and the roof. There, the twins saw the dirty, soot-covered figure of a woman behind the wall, working away at an anvil with a large hammer.

"Good morning, Windmere!" Groman called out.

Windmere turned her head, and when she saw the group, she smiled, put down her hammer, and rested her arms on the top of the wooden wall.

"Good morning, all!" she greeted them merrily. She looked over at Stephen and asked, "I assume you must be the young man I rescued last night?"

"That would be me," Stephen said. "Thanks for the assist. I'm not sure I would have made it out of that mess alive if you hadn't come along."

"I would not say that," Windmere replied with a smile. "I only saw another dozen or so of those foul things left and the single greature with a good arm. You could have taken them alone without my charging in. But you are welcome all the same. I do enjoy trampling those things from time to time."

"So Windmere, did Talrit bring the anvil out here? Or did you move it yourself when he was not looking?" Groman asked with a chuckle.

"He is picking up some more ore to smelt into tools and armor. And while he is gone, I brought the big anvil outside, where I have more room to work. It is quite tight for me inside that shop," Windmere said with a laugh as she walked out of the enclosure.

For the second time that morning, Stephen felt his jaw drop, but this time, he wasn't alone. He could see Victoria was also staring in shock. As Windmere slowly walked out from the blacksmith shop, the twins could see she was just short of seven feet tall. Her hair was tied up in a loose knot and was dark brown. She was dressed in a buckskin shirt that had been dyed a dark red color, and she also had on a large, dirty black leather apron. But what shocked the twins the most was what else they saw: instead of normal human legs, Windmere had the lower body of a horse. The horse part of her was a chestnut color that almost matched her hair and had spots of soot and dirt speckled all over it, and her tail had been pulled back into a sort of loose knot. Her horse legs had white sock-like markings that went up a few inches above her black hooves. She had some saddlebags that were strapped to her flanks, which had various tools stuffed into them. Windmere placed her hammer into one of the saddlebags, then pulled out a handkerchief from her apron pocket and wiped the soot from her face when she noticed the twin's gaze on her and sighed.

"Look, I know I need to clean up, I have been working the forge all morn...oh, I take it you have not seen a Trodontian before, have you?" she said with a wry smile as she flicked her tail out of its loose knot, letting it hang down and nearly touching the ground at its full length. "Must be quite a shock to see a creature like me for the first time."

"If you don't mind my saying so, yes," said Victoria. "In our world, we have stories of creatures like you called 'Centaurs.' But they're all myths, legends, and fairytales."

"WELL, I AM WHAT IS known here as a Trodontian, and in this world, we are no myth. But I will not deny that there are indeed some legends about us," Windmere said with a wink as she walked over to the group. "Although I am afraid I have some bad news for you, Stephen. I have been trying to fix your sword all morning to no avail."

"Wait. My sword was broken?!" Stephen said in shock he reached for where he had its sheath on his belt, only to find the sheath empty and hanging loosely at his side. "Did it happen after I was knocked out?"

"Well, when I bucked that gritter off that was trying to hitch a ride with you, your sword flew out of your hand, hit a tree, and shattered into several pieces," she said in a sad tone. "The craftsmanship, while beautiful, was more decorative than sturdy, and it was done in a way that I cannot repair, much less replicate in this shop. In my own smithy, I am certain I or my son Trakken could do it, but, as this smithy was not built with my kind in mind, I am afraid you will have to find a replacement."

Stephen looked sadly at his empty sheath hanging on his belt and sighed.

"Do not worry, Stephen. I am sure you can find a suitable weapon in the smithy," Windmere said as she walked over to Stephen and placed a hand on his shoulder. "I would go find one for you myself, but it is a challenge for me to even go inside that shop, let alone go through all the weapons. There is just not enough room for me. Just go inside and see what you can find."

"I will come with you, Stephen," Groman offered. "I have done some work for Talrit, and I know where he keeps his best weapons."

The two of them disappeared into the shop as Victoria, Falamore, and Windmere waited outside.

"So Falamore said he was a 'warrior for hire.' Are you a mercenary as well, Windmere?" Victoria asked.

"In a manner of speaking, yes, you could say I am a mercenary," Windmere answered while letting her hair down out of its knot and taking her apron off, hanging it on a peg in the smithy wall. "I prefer the term 'hired helper.' I do not normally fight for money. I just like to be able to help people who are not always able to help themselves, whether it be escorting traders across the Shadowed Plains or helping a farmer fix his plow."

"That's nice of you," Victoria said. "So where are you both from?"

"I am from Altimi, the great city in the sky to the south!" Falamore said with a flourish.

"Whereas you can find my family working our famous smithy or hunting in the forests and plains near Prariat," Windmere said as she dusted the last of the soot off her flanks.

"We were called here to train Groman, as we are some of the best in this business. But alas, we could only do so much until you arrived, lass," Falamore said.

"What do you mean?" Victoria asked. "Isn't he supposed to be a great warrior and leader?"

Victoria was interrupted by Windmere holding her finger to her mouth and motioning for her to be quiet as Groman and Stephen walked out of the smithy. Stephen had a new sword in his hands, and while it wasn't nearly as fancy as his previous one, it looked like it could take much more punishment.

"So you found a new sword, eh? Good lad!" Falamore said a little too energetically, trying to cover up what Victoria had just said.

"Do not try to be nice, Falamore," Groman said with a frown. "I heard what Victoria was saying, and I want to be the one to explain it to her."

"Explain what?" Victoria asked, puzzled.

"I do not believe fighting will fix the problems we have right now," Groman replied.

"Then explain why you have that sword on your back," Stephen countered.

Groman reached behind him and pulled the sword from its sheath. It was a large two-handed sword with a blade that split in twain two feet behind the tip. There was a gap about two inches wide between the two sides all of the way down into the hilt. On the tip of the sword the words "A TRUE LEADER" were inscribed.

"This is the Empty Sword. This is what 'The Chosen One' is destined to wield. And I plan to only use it for the defense of my village. I want no part in galivanting all over the land and slaughtering dozens of gritters and greatures just for the fun of it. On top of that, I have never been trained how to use it in battle, nor will I be taught. I was taught to heal and help others, and now, if you will excuse me, it is high time I go back to the healer's house to assist him in his morning duties," he said as he returned the elegant weapon to its sheath and walked away in a huff.

"That wasn't what I was expecting at all," Victoria said.

Windmere looked at Groman as he disappeared around a corner. "This is the challenge we have run into. I cannot say I blame him, though. He has had a lot of responsibility thrust upon his shoulders. And fighting is not something the Kittrian are known for," she added with a sigh.

"I'll say. Tori and I took on two Kittrian guards in Tredut on our first day here. We were completely unarmed, and we were still able to defeat them rather easily," Stephen said with a laugh.

"Aye, lad. Kittrians are known for their peaceful nature. That is why Windmere and I are here. When we learned of The Chosen One's reluctance to fight, we changed tactics. We now use Areiop as a center for our campaigns against the Shadowed One's forces," Falamore said. "Now, Windmere, I think it is time we show the lad and lass our strategy for dealing with those pests. On to the meeting hall!" he said with a shout as he stretched out his wings and with one flap, he took off into the sky.

Windmere sighed and stared up after him. "He never stays on the ground for more than an hour. You would think he was allergic to it." She chuckled.

"He does seem a bit high up in the air, doesn't he?" Victoria quipped.

The three heroes laughed for a minute before stopping themselves when they heard a loud screech coming from above.

"Uh oh. Do you think he heard that?" Stephen said.

"That was not Falamore's call. It sounded more like Vulant, Falamore's adopted son. He has been out on patrol since daybreak," Windmere said.

Just then, another different call echoed overhead, and Windmere looked up in surprise.

"That is the signal of a raid! We need to get to the meeting hall right away! Hop on! I will take you both there!" Windmere shouted as Stephen and Victoria scrambled onto the Trodontian's back and held on tightly as she took off at a gallop towards the meeting hall.

Chapter 5. Raiding the Raiders.

Windmere skidded to a stop in front of the meeting hall, Stephen and Victoria jumped off her back, and the three of them went inside. Victoria could see Falamore and Groman standing over a large map on a table. There was also an elderly Kittrian man, whom she assumed to be the village elder, and another Blakmian, like Falamore, only he was slightly shorter, and his wings and feathers were much more of a golden-brown color with black tips, and his tail was a more red color.

The Blakmian seemed to be pointing out a spot on the map to the group.

"I just spotted a large group of gritters being led by three greatures getting ready to attack Lapik!" the Blakmian shouted. "There are a few hundred gritters, and if my guess is correct, they will attack at sundown."

"Those monsters!" the elder said, shocked. "Lapik is only a tiny fishing village, with only a handful of armed guards to defend it! We must do something!"

"Aye, sir. But I feel that we three are too few to deal with this new threat," Falamore said as he looked up and saw Windmere and the twins entering the hall.

"We can handle them," Stephen said boldly as he walked into the center of the room. Victoria and Windmere looked at him in surprise.

"But you were wounded! When I brought you in last night, you were hardly in any condition to fight," Windmere said.

"I'm feeling better by the minute. Besides, I want a rematch with those gritters," Stephen said. "So are you with us or not?"

"I'm in," Victoria said, walking forward to join her brother in the center of the room.

"I am sure with all of us, it will be an easy thing to win the day," Windmere said as she trotted into the center of the room and stood near the map table.

"Aye, my friend. I and my son Vulant will be ready to assist you," Falamore said as he and his son joined the group in the middle of the room.

Groman looked at the heroes, rolled his eyes, and sighed.

"I already told you: I will not aid you in mindlessly slaughtering those creatures. Good day," he said loudly as he pushed past the group, causing some of them to move out of the way, with Windmere accidentally knocking over a table behind her in the process. Groman ignored the mess and swiftly left the meeting hall.

The elder mumbled something along the lines of: "I will talk to him. Good luck, and may The One Above be with you." And left the hall as well.

After they were gone, Victoria and Windmere began to clean up the mess the latter had accidentally made, while Stephen walked over to the map.

"So where is the enemy located?" Stephen asked.

Vulant swiftly strode over and pointed to a marking below a large lake. "The village of Lapik is located on the southern side of Forrest Lake. And our target is encamped on the western side of the village," he replied.

"Well, do you have any ideas on how to deal with a small army of three-foot-high monsters who can gut you like a fish?" Victoria asked.

"I'm not sure," Stephen replied. He thought for a moment and looked up at the three mercenaries standing nearby. "How have you dealt with these kinds of threats before?" he asked.

"We have not," Windmere responded. "Until now, we have only dealt with small raiding parties that normally don't have any more than fifty gritters. This is the largest force we have seen in a long while."

Stephen went back to the map and started looking it over again. "How do those gritters normally fight? Last night, they only seemed to just swarm us with no rhyme or reason. Do they take orders from someone or something?" he asked.

"Aye, lad. The greatures are normally the fiends in charge of the little monsters," Falamore answered.

"So what would happen if we killed all the greatures in charge of that army?" Stephen asked.

"Normally, when you kill one greature, another will take charge if there is one nearby," Vulant said.

"So what if we take them all out simultaneously? Will the gritters become disorganized and retreat?" Stephen pressed.

"That has been my experience with those pests," Windmere said.

"Alright, then. How about Windmere, Victoria, and I keep the gritters busy on the ground, while Falamore and Vulant stay in the air, find the greatures, and kill them as soon as you spot them? Hopefully, we can hold out long enough for you to eliminate all the leaders," Stephen said.

"That sounds like a capable strategy, lad," Falamore said.

"I think it will work," Vulant agreed.

"It is settled, then. Let us go gather our weapons and prepare for the fight," Windmere said as she carefully turned around, trying to not knock anything else over, and the five warriors left the meeting hall together.

AFTER HEADING BACK to the smithy and finding suitable armor and weapons for themselves, the twins were soon riding on Windmere's back once more, as they moved across the open plains at a swift pace, and the sun began to set. Victoria looked behind her at her brother, who was hanging on tightly to her back as they rode. He had a metal chest plate, gauntlets, helmet, and metal plates on his legs. He had not one but two one-handed swords in their sheaths, bouncing at his sides. She, too, was wearing armor nearly identical to his, but she was wearing the special armored boots and gauntlets she had gotten from the smithy on their second day there. Her decorative Kittrian sword hung in its sheath at her side, and she also had a large shield attached to her backplate.

"How much longer until we get there?!" she shouted to Windmere between strides.

Windmere turned her head and looked back at her without changing her pace.

"We are nearly at where Vulant said the gritters were encamped," she replied. "Look up and see if you can spot Falamore or Vulant. They will signal us when they have the enemy in sight."

Stephen looked up and scanned the sky; he saw the golden black-tipped wings of Vulant soaring high above them. Suddenly, he spotted Falamore's golden wings as he completed a graceful loop.

He looked back at his sister and Windmere and kicked the latter's sides. Windmere skidded to a stop and bucked, throwing Stephen off, while Victoria managed to hang on. Stephen landed in the tall grass on his back, and he lay there for a bit, while he tried to get air in his lungs again. Windmere trotted over to him, with Victoria still on her back.

"What was that for, young man?!" Windmere nearly shouted angrily.

Stephen coughed and struggled to his feet.

"I saw Falamore give the signal that we're close to the camp. I thought that was the way I was to let you know."

"You were supposed to just tell me. Not kick me!" Windmere snorted as Victoria slid off and walked over to the top of a nearby hill.

"Quiet, you two!" Victoria hissed. "I can see the camp from here."

Stephen hurried over to the top of the hill and looked over. He could see three of what looked to be lean-tos made out of animal skins dotted around a large area below them. He saw that there were indeed hundreds of gritters scurrying about, getting ready for their assault on the village.

The twins turned around and walked back to Windmere, who was busy strapping on her own armor and two large hand-and-a-half swords.

"What is your plan, then?" Windmere asked as she pulled out a helmet from her saddlebags.

"Well, that looks like a hornet's nest just waiting to be stirred up. But we're too few to handle a full-on swarm. Victoria and I will try to lure the gritters away a few at a time to lessen their numbers. When we start to get overrun, we'll signal you to come charging in and help us out," Stephen replied.

"A good plan," Victoria said as she pulled her shield from its place on her back and slipped her left arm into the handles.

"Agreed. What will your signal be?" Windmere asked.

"Listen for Tori to bang her sword against her shield three times," Stephen said.

Windmere and Victoria nodded in agreement, and the twins began to climb the hill once more, staying low in the tall grass. They crept towards the camp as quietly as their armor would allow. Once they could hear the screeches and growls of the gritters, they stopped.

"Here's what we can do: let's make a little noise and see if we can get some of the gritters to investigate," Stephen whispered, and Victoria nodded her approval.

Stephen found a large stone and tossed it into the air above them, and it landed nearby. At once, the twins could hear the gritters screeching and begin to move towards them. Suddenly, three gritters appeared in the grass in front of the twins and froze in surprise. The twins lowered the visors on their helmets, drew their swords, and lunged at the gritters, but before they could finish them, the lead gritter let out a wail before its head was removed from its body. The twins quickly dealt with the remaining two before they heard a cry come up from the camp and the sound of dozens of gritters beginning to swarm toward them.

"We weren't fast enough! Now, the whole camp knows we're here. Should I signal now?!" Victoria shouted, her voice echoing in her helmet.

"Not yet!" Stephen replied as he began to cut away at the arriving gritters with his swords.

Victoria saw a gritter leap at her, and she thrust out her shield towards him and knocked him aside, only to see more of them coming at her. Victoria started swinging her sword from side to side, felling gritters by the score.

As they kept fighting, they heard a roar from the camp that faded into a moan, then it died out completely.

"There goes one of the leaders!" Stephen shouted above the noise of battle.

"There's too many of them, now!" Victoria shouted as more and more gritters showed up.

"Then, do it!" Stephen replied as he sliced two more gritters in half with one swing.

Victoria swatted the attacking gritters aside and beat her sword on her shield three times. She then smacked another gritter with her shield and soon could hear Windmere charging into the fray.

Windmere smashed into the horde of gritters at a full gallop, throwing them aside like they were toys and carving a path deep into the enemy camp with her swords. The twins then heard another greature getting killed from within the camp, and they began to see gritters turning away and fleeing into the sunset. Suddenly, they heard a deafening roar from their left, and they turned to see the hulking figure of a greature, wielding a large club, barreling towards them.

The greature was just over six feet and had stone grey skin and glowing red eyes. He had a large mouth full of triangular teeth and a tiny nose. He wore a rough metal breastplate over ragged clothing and was swinging a fallen tree trunk as a club.

Victoria had barely enough time to raise her shield when the brute's club hit it, and the force of the blow made her slide back a few feet on the grass soaked with grey blood from slain gritters. Victoria had to turn her attention to the gritters that had now begun to rally and swarm towards her again. Stephen saw the brute send his sister sliding backward and raised his swords in a defensive posture. The brute swung his club, and Stephen dodged with ease, slashing the beast's leg with his sword.

The brute slid to a stop and looked at him in surprise.

"You! You are the one I almost killed last night! You will not be so fortunate this time!" the greature snarled as he attempted to charge at Stephen once again.

"Bring it on, you coward!" Stephen shouted back as the greature roared and staggered towards him, raising its club over its head to strike a deadly blow, but Stephen was ready. He had his swords in an x-shaped posture, and when the greature was close enough, he pulled his swords apart and cleanly cut the monster's head and arms off. The lifeless corpse sank to its knees and fell over as Stephen stepped away from it to avoid getting crushed. Almost as if a radio signal went off, all the gritters stopped what they were doing, looked at the fallen greature, and fled away into the sunset.

As the twins watched their retreating foes run away, Windmere galloped up to them and slid to a stop. Her armor and legs were covered with grey blood, and she was breathing hard, but she was smiling.

"That was a fine fight. Well done, you two!" she said breathlessly as she pulled off her helmet.

Just then, Falamore and Vulant swooped down and landed next to the trio.

"Aye, young warriors. Thou hast fought well. Victory indeed belongs to us," Falamore said with a smile.

"Sorry I was not able to hit that last greature, Stephen," Vulant said. "He was darting in and out among the trees, and I had trouble getting a clear shot."

"That's fine with me. I got to have my revenge for that log last night. That brute said he was the one who attacked Victoria and me," Stephen replied as he knelt to wipe his swords on the grass.

"So we've won?" Victoria asked as she wiped off her shield and sword with a rag.

"Aye, lass. That we have," Falamore said, "for now, anyway. It is only a matter of time before they regroup and attack some other town. We must remain vigilant if we are to protect the villages."

"I agree that we need to always be ready for another attack, but I do not think that we are in any more danger tonight. Let us go to Lapik and see if we can stay the night. I am too tired to walk all of the way back to Areiop," Windmere said as she gathered up her things.

After a brief rest and cleaning off their armor and weapons, the warriors turned east and soon found themselves in a cozy inn inside the tiny town of Lapik. After taking turns cleaning up in a wooden washtub, the twins saw that they had been put into the same room. They were a little annoyed at this, but they were too tired to say anything. When they saw the two beds on either side of the room separated by a curtain, they wordlessly flopped down on the beds and were soon sound asleep.

They didn't wake up until the next morning, when a message flew through the window and landed on Stephen's face.

Chapter 6. Spearhead.

"Get it off! Get it off! Get! It! Off!"

Stephen's screams jolted Victoria from her slumber. In one fluid motion, she sprang from her bed and pulled her sword from its sheath, pulled back the dividing curtain, and was about to strike whatever was attacking Stephen when she saw what her brother's assailant actually was. It looked like a lizard, but it had six legs and fleshy wings that it was flapping wildly to try and maintain its hold on Stephen's panicked face.

Victoria walked over, gently picked up the lizard, and found it had a piece of rolled-up paper tied to its tail. After gently pulling the paper off, she put the lizard on the ground, where it quickly scurried over to the window, climbed up to it, and took off into the sunny sky.

"What was that thing?" Stephen asked as he climbed out of bed.

Victoria unrolled the paper and read the message:

Stephen and Victoria,

I received word of your triumph this morning, and I wanted to congratulate you on a job well done. When you are able, please return to Areiop as soon as possible. There are things we must discuss.

Elder Gilder.

"That was fast. Those lizards must move quickly," Victoria remarked as she rolled up the paper and put it in her pack.

"Gives a whole new meaning of 'air mail,' eh?" Stephen said jokingly.

Victoria turned to look out of the open window. "Oh, hey, it's coming back," she commented.

Stephen quickly stole a panicked look out the window and turned beet red when Victoria burst out laughing. He glared at her as she laughed her way out of the room before sheepishly following.

After a bountiful breakfast that consisted of fried fish, meat, and vegetables, the victorious group made their way back along the lake towards Areiop once more.

Upon their arrival, they were greeted at the gate by a tall Kittrian man, who waved them over. Falamore and Vulant landed, while Windmere trotted over to him, and the twins dismounted. The Kittrian man was well dressed in colorful robes but also had a gleaming sword in its sheath at his side.

"Greetings. I am Inola, captain of the village guard and the commander of the local militia. I wanted to catch you as soon as I could. I have news of another possible attack. We received word from a Trodontian scout of a large force of gritters and greatures gathering to the southwest of Prariat. Their numbers seem to be larger than the army that you stopped last night."

"That is my home! My children are still there!" Windmere shouted. "We must leave at once!"

The twins quickly remounted, and the two birdmen rocketed back into the air.

"We will fly ahead and alert the Prariat militia! We shall meet you west of the city!" Vulant shouted from above.

Windmere took off into Areiop at a gallop, and the trio could see the Areiop smithy fast approaching and Groman waiting for them in front of it.

"I have packed some things for your trip!" he shouted as he tossed two leather bags at the group. Windmere barely even slowed down as the twins on her back caught the bags and they raced past.

After getting their supplies, they rounded a corner and found themselves racing through a marketplace. Windmere did her best to avoid the villagers and their stalls, but she spotted a cartload of round reddish vegetables that was directly in her path.

"Hold on!" she shouted as she leaped over the cart. Unfortunately, her back hooves caught the edge of the cart, causing it to topple over and spill its load. Windmere stumbled but kept going, as the shopkeeper ran outside.

"No! My Karotos! Come back here and pay for those, you clumsy Trodontian!" He shouted at them.

"Sorry!" Windmere shouted back as she left him in her dust.

The twins held on as Windmere continued to race toward her home. The city soon gave way to the forest as they were back into another tree-lined tunnel, which then gave way to open grassland with trees dotted about.

After about an hour of hard riding, they came to a small river where Windmere finally came to a stop.

"I need to stop for a moment. Can you two swim?" she asked the twins, nearly out of breath.

"We can both swim, but I'm not sure about crossing that river with all this gear and armor," Victoria said.

"Put whatever you cannot swim with in my saddlebags. I can handle it; I once crossed this river with an anvil in my arms," Windmere said, panting.

"Really?" Stephen asked with a shocked look.

"Not exactly. It was only a little one I got from the ice dwarves of the Northern Ice Range," she admitted. "I was transporting it to Areiop for trading. Ice Dwarf weapons and tools are really valuable over there."

The twins chuckled and placed their armor and weapons in Windmere's saddlebags. They then dove into the cold water, and, once they found that the current wasn't too strong, they crossed the river in a few minutes. They then laid out on the grassy shore and let the sun dry them as they waited for Windmere to catch her breath and cross the river.

After about twenty minutes, Windmere finally joined them on the other side, and they were soon on their way again, albeit at a slower pace.

In the late afternoon, they crested a hill and saw a large group of Trodontians, all of whom were armed to the teeth and covered in armor and chain mail. When they saw Windmere and the twins, they cheered and held their left arms against their chests in salute. Then, one of the Trodontians, who seemed to be taller than the rest came forward and was about to speak when Windmere interrupted him.

"Have they attacked yet, Clydesat?"

"Not yet, thank The One Above," he replied in a deep voice. "And Saralia and Trakken are safe as well. Saralia had left on one of her northern hunting trips this morning, and Trakken is scouting the enemy with the two Blakmians as we speak."

Just then, Falamore and Vulant swooped in and landed next to the group, and a Trodontian trotted over to Windmere, who, upon seeing him, spun around so fast the twins fell off her back, and she galloped over to him and hugged him.

"Trakken! I am so glad to see you are safe!" she said.

"It is good to see you too, Mother!" Trakken said.

Stephen and Victoria looked over at the happy reunion, and, despite their hard landing, they couldn't help but smile.

Trakken looked over at the twins and walked over.

"So you must be the two of the three 'Chosen Ones'? I'm honored to finally meet you," he said.

Stephen looked over their new friend. He was slightly taller than Windmere at seven feet and more muscular; his skin and his horse half were a darker color, but his face had the same warm smile as his mother. He was dressed in full plate armor and was armed with two war hammers, one hanging on each side, and a large two-handed sword hanging on his left flank.

However, Falamore's booming voice interrupted Stephen's train of thought.

"The foul beasts are marching towards Prariat as we speak! We have only a half-hour before they arrive at the gates! We must attack now!"

"What is our plan?!" one of the Trodontian soldiers shouted back.

"That is up to The Chosen Ones to decide. They were brought here to finish this war against The Shadowed One, and so they shall!" another Trodontian replied.

At this, all eyes turned on Stephen and Victoria, who stood silently nearby. After a few seconds, Stephen stepped forward.

"How many fighters do we have?" he asked.

"Our numbers are just over one hundred," came the commander's reply.

"And how many gritters and greatures are we dealing with?"

"We estimate nearly seven hundred gritters and a hundred greatures in the center of the army."

"So the odds are in our favor, then? Good," Stephen said as he rubbed his chin and began to pace back and forth, deep in thought. After a minute, he turned back to the assembled army. "Alright! Here is my plan! We will have Falamore, Vulant, and about twenty soldiers race ahead and try to lure the army away from Prariat. They will keep their distance but keep the enemy focused on them and hopefully get the pests to follow them. Falamore and Vulant can provide protection from any gritters that manage to get too close with their longbows. In the meantime, the rest of us will be moving into a position to strike at the enemy's rear. We will form a tight spearhead formation and charge into the enemy as deep as we can, focusing on taking out the greature commanders. From what I have seen, the gritters are controlled through a sort of hive mind, like a swarm of bugs. Once we take out the commanders, the gritters will run away, and we will have won the day once more!"

The army was quiet for a moment before Trakken stepped forward.

"Well, Clydesat, what are we waiting for? Gather your nineteen soldiers and prepare for battle!" Trakken shouted.

At this, a cheer came from the soldiers, and immediately, there was chaos as the soldiers gathered their weapons and armor and prepared for the fight ahead. The twins kept having to move aside to keep from getting themselves trampled in the madness.

Suddenly, Stephen felt himself being gripped by a rough pair of strong arms, and he was lifted onto Trakken's back, while Victoria found herself once again on Windmere.

"Prepare yourself. The battle will begin soon!" Windmere shouted above the noise.

The twins soon donned their armor and weapons, and once the army was ready, they got into position on top of a tall hill. From there, they could see the army of gritters and greatures below them slowly moving towards their intended target.

After a few minutes, they saw Clydesat and his group attack the front of the army and then turn away and quickly gallop to the gritter's right flank. Just as Stephen hoped, the gritters and greatures gave chase, and the entire army was soon running after the small group with their backs towards the larger army that was still hidden on top of the hill.

"Now, men! For Prariat!!!" Windmere bellowed as she and Trakken began to gallop down the hillside at top speed while the twins hung on for dear life, and the rest of the army charged right behind them.

The army assembled into a wedge formation as they grew closer to the enemy forces. When they were thirty feet away, some of the gritters at the back of the enemy army began to turn around while they were still giving chase, only to look on in horror as the armored force smashed into them like a battering ram. Windmere and Trakken barely slowed down as gritters were thrown aside or trampled under their hooves. The twins would take a swipe at the gritters when they were able, but they mostly just held on as the Trodontian army continued even deeper into the seething mass of gritters. Then, the hulking figures of the greatures rose up from the masses, and some of them began to turn towards their attackers, wielding large clubs, maces, spears, and a few shields. The greatures who had noticed the rapidly-approaching army raised their weapons and shields in an effort to defend themselves, but it was already too late. Windmere and Victoria cut two down within seconds, barely even slowing down, and Trakken smashed two greatures with his war hammers, while Stephen was kept busy, trying to keep the gritters from swarming them.

The Trodontians' charge began to slow down as more and more greatures began to turn around and fight back; soon, the army was at a near standstill as the greatures had now begun to push back, and the Trodontian army soon found itself boxed in by the remaining gritters and greatures. The soldiers were desperately trying to keep from getting swarmed by the gritters when suddenly, a hail of arrows began to rain down on the greatures, dropping them left and right. And just like the night before, as the greatures fell, more and more gritters began to turn and flee as their masters died. The Trodontians cheered as they began to press forward again, as the familiar screeches of Falamore's and Vulant's war cries echoed around them. Soon, the last greature was dead on the ground, bleeding from an arrow in its neck and a gash from Victoria's sword in its belly.

After they had confirmed the enemy was either dead or had run away, the Trodontian army regrouped at the northern side of the battlefield. Clydesat came over to Windmere, Trakken, and the twins, who by this time had dismounted and were cleaning their weapons.

"The battle is won! And not a single soldier has died today!" Clydesat said ecstatically.

"That is indeed good news! Are we to head back to Prariat now?" Trakken asked as he shook the last bits of greature off his war hammers.

"I would hope we are! I wager that Saralia has an epic feast awaiting our arrival. We should not keep it waiting!" Windmere said with a laugh.

"My men and I will take care of the cleanup. We shall send for you if we need you. Go be with your family and your new friends," Clydesat said with a smile.

With that, Windmere and Trakken picked up their human comrades and took off at a gallop northward.

Within twenty minutes, the twins could see their destination; it was a city much larger than the Kittrian villages they had seen before. There was a wooden stockade-like wall surrounding the city, and the houses also seemed to be made of wood, with some having thatched roofs, while others had wooden shingles. As they approached, Windmere and Trakken slowed down to a walk, and the twins could see two huge wooden gates swing open, and some armored guards stepped out and stood on either side of the entrance. Upon seeing Windmere and Trakken, they gave the Trodontian salute and stepped aside, allowing the four of them inside.

Once inside, the twins could see a bustling city full of Trodontians going about their daily lives. Some of the other Trodontians looked up at the newcomers, but most didn't pay them much attention.

Soon, the group came to a large house that the twins assumed belonged to Windmere and her family. It was nearly two stories tall and had a large open-air blacksmith shop in front of it and a covered patio area to the left. Windmere and Trakken came to a stop in front of the house, and the twins dismounted.

"I am going to go see if Saralia is in the smokehouse around back. Once I return, we can have some dinner," Windmere said as she walked away.

"Come on. Let me show you around our house," Trakken said as he led the twins into the enclosed smithy.

All the tools a blacksmith could ever want were scattered around on workbenches and hanging on pegs. Several large forges were facing the house and multiple anvils nearby. The walls had dozens of different kinds of weapons in varying degrees of completion hanging on the walls.

Victoria began to look around the workbenches, while Stephen walked over to the door that led into the house. It was a two-part door that one could open the top half or bottom half, or both if one preferred. As he got closer, Stephen noticed the scent of seemed like roasted venison. His hunger got the better of him, and he quietly opened the door and snuck inside when Trakken and Victoria weren't looking.

"So your sister likes to hunt?" Victoria asked Trakken as she looked over a large, intricately engraved dagger.

"Oh, yes. She is quite good at it, too. Why, one day...." Trakken began to answer but was interrupted by a girl's scream and the sound of two metal objects hitting one another.

All at once, the door burst open, and Stephen came flying out, hitting a workbench on his way down and nearly knocking it over in the process. Victoria hurried over to her brother, who was lying on the ground and clearly had the wind knocked out of him. She could also see the clear imprints of two horseshoes in the center of his breastplate.

Suddenly, a young female Trodontian wearing a tan deerskin shirt and a long brown leather apron burst through the door, looking very angry. She had long blond hair that was in a long braid down her back, and her horse half was a very pale tan.

"Chosen Ones or not, *nobody* touches the food before it is ready!" she shouted.

Trakken laughed and said, "Victoria, meet Saralia, my younger sister. It would appear your brother has already met her."

Chapter 7. Tales and Legends.

Victoria helped her brother to his feet as Windmere came rushing over.

"What was that noise?!" she yelled as she came into view, then she stopped and surveyed the scene.

"Mother, he tried to take some of the food before I could finish it, so I gave him a light kick to get him to stop," Saralia said defensively.

"That was a light kick?" Stephen groaned as he removed his now-dented breastplate.

"I might have put some more power into it than I had intended. I am not used to dealing with thieves on the smaller side," Saralia said as she looked over at Trakken, who turned a slight shade of red. She went back inside and soon returned with a clay jar filled with a greenish paste.

"Here, try rubbing this on the bruise. It will ease the pain," Saralia said with an awkward smile.

Stephen took the jar, dipped his finger in it, took out a small amount, and rubbed it on his chest under his tunic. As soon as he did, he could feel the pain begin to go away.

"Thanks," he said quietly. "Sorry for trying to snitch some food earlier."

Saralia smirked and nodded, then took the jar and went back inside the house. Trakken took Stephen's damaged breastplate, walked over to a workbench, and began to examine it, while Windmere shook her head before following her daughter inside the house.

Victoria looked at Stephen, who was now sitting down on an anvil.

"Did she sneak up on you?" she asked in a whisper.

"Not really. Her back was to me, and I thought I could get past her and grab a small piece of the meat on the counter behind her," he whispered.

"You dummy!" Victoria said quietly as she gave his shoulder a shove. "Don't you know never to approach a horse from behind?"

"I do now," Stephen mumbled.

Trakken began to beat out the dents in Stephen's armor on one of the anvils when the top half of the door opened, and Windmere poked her head out.

"Dinner is ready!" she called.

Just then, Falamore and Vulant swooped down and landed outside.

"Oh, good, you are here!" Windmere said. "Come in! We have more than enough food for everybody!"

Soon, the warriors had cleaned up, and the two-legged ones were seated around a table. Victoria couldn't help but look around at the building they were in. Although it had looked like a two-story edifice from the outside, it was actually made of only one. A large cookstove was in the corner in what seemed to be a kitchen that was attached to the room they were in. There were a few adjoining rooms separated by the same two-piece door that was outside. Everything seemed larger and more spaced apart than the Kittrian houses, but she figured it was because of the Trodontians' size.

Their meal consisted of large portions of grilled meat with roasted herbs and vegetables. Soon, she, her brother, and the Blakmians had eaten their fill, but the three Trodontians were still cleaning their plates.

"That was an awesome battle today," Stephen said with a sigh as he leaned back in his chair.

"Aye, lad. It was indeed a glorious victory!" Falamore agreed and took another drink from his earthen cup.

"Something just doesn't add up, though," Victoria said quietly.

"What do you mean?" Vulant asked.

"Doesn't it seem like those gritters attacking here right after we defeated them in Lapik is a bit too coincidental?" Victoria wondered aloud.

"How so?" Stephen questioned, leaning forward and resting his arms on the table.

"It's almost like they went straight from Lapik to the fields outside of Prariat."

"Lass, there are numerous gritters; there have been raids occurring quite often," Falamore said quietly.

"I can see that, but what if they are just moving to a different target after we chase them off from the first one?" Victoria countered.

"That greature from Lapik did say he was a part of the group that attacked us on the way to Areiop," Stephen said.

"Exactly! That could be two times we have seen them do this!" Victoria said excitedly.

"So you are saying that every time we beat those things back, they just regroup with another greature and more gritters and then attack somewhere else?" Windmere asked, looking up from her dinner.

"Yes," Victoria replied. She then looked over at Falamore and Vulant. "Did you see if the gritters were running in any specific direction today?" she asked.

"Now that you mention it, the majority of them did seem to be heading towards the south," Vulant said.

"Is there a city to the south of us?" Stephen said.

"There is one directly south of us: Altimi. It is nearly a three-day journey at a normal pace; one at top speed." Windmere said.

"Isn't that where you're both from?" Victoria asked the two Blakmians.

"Aye, lass. And I do not plan to go there again," Falamore said with a frown as he stood up from the table and walked outside.

The twins looked on in surprise, while Vulant sighed and looked back at the twins.

"Why won't he go back to his home city?" Stephen asked.

"Long ago, our great king, known as 'The Golden One,' died, leaving his only son, the prince, as an heir. The prince either could not or would not handle the responsibility, and he disappeared. He has not been seen or heard from since then. Now, the northern half of the city is empty, and the people have no leader. Because of that, many of them have become mercenaries, and what remains of Altimi actually seems to be flourishing, despite the lack of a king," Vulant explained.

"So how does your father fit into all of this?" Victoria asked.

"He doesn't say much to me about it, but I know he was close to the king when he died, and he feels that the prince betrayed his people when he left. Since then, he does not like to even get close to Altimi," Vulant replied.

"Well, if we're right, and that is their next target, do you think he will come with us?" Stephen asked.

"I cannot say for certain. I have tried to talk to him about it, but he will not listen to me."

"I'll go talk to him. You should work on a strategy on how we should deal with those pests if they are there," Victoria said as she got up and went outside into the late evening air, while Vulant looked at Stephen in concern.

"I doubt she will be able to convince him to return," Vulant said quietly.

"You don't know my sister," Stephen said with a weak smile. He then started asking Vulant more questions about Altimi and forging their plans for the battle ahead.

VICTORIA WALKED THROUGH the enclosed smithy and looked around, trying to find Falamore, but he was nowhere to be seen. She then went outside into the roadway in front of the house. A passing Trodontian farmer pulling a wagon saw her and waved, and she gave a quick wave in response.

Then, she heard a noise from above her and saw Falamore sitting on top of the wooden roof of the house, working on some arrow shafts. Wasting no time, she ran over, jumped on top of a nearby barrel, and grabbed the edge of the roof and with one swing managed to get herself on top of it. She then carefully climbed up beside the Blakmian warrior and quietly sat down next to him.

"Your climbing skills are impressive, lass," he said quietly as he gazed into the dying light of the sunset.

"I'm told I can climb like a cat," she said.

"I beg your pardon?"

"It's a small creature in my world we sometimes keep as a pet."

"Ah, well, I assume you are here to change my mind on returning to my old home."

"Not exactly. I wanted to ask you why you don't want to go back there to begin with."

"Lass, I know my son told you already."

"But some things just don't add up. I can understand thinking the prince was a traitor, and he did mention the whole northern side of the city was abandoned, but he also said that what was left of the city was flourishing now. Isn't that a good thing?"

"Aye, lass. In one way, it could seem like that it is a beneficial thing for my people to not have a ruler, but what do you think they have done in his stead?"

"I honestly have no idea."

Falamore stood up from his spot and balanced on the peak of the roof.

"It is near anarchy there, now! The whole city is a den of thieves, mercenaries, and thugs. The only reason the city seems to be prospering now is because of the black market, which has been growing ever since the prince left. And now all I can do is watch it happen."

"I'm sorry to hear that. Are you sure there is nothing you can do?"

"Aye, lass. I have kept in touch with some friends who still live in the city, and they said that they think that even if the prince returned, it is likely not everyone will listen to him nor follow his word."

Victoria thought for a moment and looked up at Falamore.

"Why did the prince leave? Vulant said you were close to the king when he died. Did you see the prince leave as well?"

Falamore sighed and sat back down next to Victoria.

"Aye, lass. I was the last one to see him before he left. He told me that he was sorry, but he did not think he was fit to rule until he could figure some things out on his own. That was over ten years ago, and nobody has heard from him since."

"I see. So, do you think he will ever return?"

"When the time is right, he will appear in royal armor in the hall of the king, and he will claim his rightful place on the throne. That is what the letter to his people said."

"If Steve and I are right about Altimi being the next target, maybe the right time is now. If they are attacked, they are going to need a leader. Maybe you can just fill in for him until he returns?"

Falamore let out another sigh.

"Lass, while you may be right about the city in the sky being the next target, I cannot bring myself to return to that place until the prince has been found."

"I understand, but you need to think about this: your people may need you soon, and we shouldn't abandon our own," Victoria said. She then got up and began to carefully climb back down from the roof. She was almost to the edge when a loud crash from inside startled her, and she slipped and began to fall.

Before she tumbled off the roof, she felt two strong limbs grab her shoulders, and she began to rise into the air. She looked up to see Falamore had grabbed her with his feet and was now soaring into the night sky. He swung her forward, caught her with his hands, and gently moved her to his back just between his huge bronze wings.

Victoria had been in a few airplanes before, and even a hot air balloon once, but this was an entirely new experience. The cold night air blew in her face and made her hair stream out behind her like a flag. She could see the entirety of the city below them, the great plains beyond, and a large mountain range to their right. She looked up and saw the sky was full of stars and the three moons glowing in a spectacular brilliance.

"This is beautiful!" she said over the noise of the wind in her face.

"Aye, lass. That it is," Falamore replied, turning his head to look at his passenger as he set his wings in a soaring position.

After flying in silence for a few minutes, Falamore spoke up.

"I have thought about what you have said. Those foul beasts will most likely make their camp on the cliffside passageway or in the abandoned part of the city. I will aid your efforts there but no further."

Victoria leaned forward and wrapped her hands around Falamore's neck to better hold on, and she whispered in his ear: "Thank you, Falamore."

The two of them began to descend in a graceful spiral until they reached the ground. Victoria dropped to the earth, her boots making a soft thud on the packed dirt of the roadway. Falamore smiled at her and took off into the night again. Victoria looked up at the rapidly-shrinking figure.

"That was incredible. Thank you," she whispered into the night air.

She then turned and walked into the house, where she saw Windmere and Trakken arm wrestling on the table, and everyone else was cheering one or the other on. They didn't notice her walk over to a window and look out once more at the three moons glowing in the night sky.

"Perhaps Steve was right for once. This has been an incredible adventure so far. I hope it only gets better from here," she mused quietly to herself as she heard a cheer erupt from behind her. She turned as Trakken managed to win the round and start prancing around the room like a trained pony. She joined in the group's laughter and watched with amusement as her brother then challenged Saralia in another arm-wrestling match and was swiftly and soundly defeated.

Chapter 8. An Uphill Battle.

Stephen awoke in a hammock to his roommate's snoring.

He looked over at Trakken, who was sleeping while standing up. His human torso was leaning into some sort of harness, and he was snoring away like a chainsaw. Stephen got up and quietly walked out of the bedroom, across the main chamber, and out into the smithy, where, to his surprise, he found Victoria at one of the workbenches.

"Good morning, Tori," he said with a yawn.

"Hi, Steve," came her quiet reply.

"What are you working on?"

"Oh, just something I saw a picture of in one of the books you like to read."

Stephen looked closer and saw a sketch of an unusual weapon by most standards but a familiar one to him. They were known as Tekko-Kagi, a type of ancient Japanese weapon used by various ninja clans. They were a set of between two to four metal claws that extended from a metal handle and leather strap that was fastened to the user's wrist and forearm.

"Tekko-Kagi?" Stephen asked.

"I think they may work better with my fighting style, and since we are at the house of expert blacksmiths, I want to see if either Windmere or Trakken can make some," Victoria responded.

"Did I hear my name?" asked Windmere with a yawn as she exited the house and walked over to the twins.

"I was wondering if you could try and make something for me before we leave for Altimi. It's a kind of weapon we have seen in our world, and I think they may work better for me than a sword," Victoria said, holding up her sketch and handing it to Windmere, who took it and looked it over.

"Hmmm. That is definitely not a weapon I am familiar with, but I am sure Trakken and I can have a set ready by the time we move out. Let me just wake Trakken and Saralia up, and we can get started."

Windmere walked over to a large bucket of water and took it inside. The twins waited in silence for a moment and then heard a splash of water along with Trakken shouting from inside.

"Mother! What was that for?!"

The twins then heard a muffled conversation from inside, and within a few minutes, a wet and disheveled Trakken came outside, grumbling to himself and pulling on a dry leather shirt. He looked over at the twins and yawned.

"Mother says you have a project for me?" Trakken asked as he donned a large heavy apron and walked over to Victoria.

"I was wondering if you could make a pair of these for me," Victoria said, holding out the sketch of the weapon. Trakken took it and looked it over for a minute before placing it on one of the workbenches.

"This is an intriguing design. I have a bunch of old knives and other small blades I can reuse for these...what do you call them?"

"In our world, they are called Tekko-Kagi. They were mostly used by stealth fighters and martial artists, as they attach to the user's wrist and forearm. They can aid in hand-to-hand combat as well as climbing," Stephen responded.

"Sounds like something an Amronian could make good use of. Victoria, did you want me to add these to your gauntlets or build them on their own?" Trakken asked as he brought a large wooden box down from a shelf and opened it up to reveal a large assortment of blades and broken weapons.

"Could you make them so I can wear them with or without the gauntlets on?" Victoria asked.

"That should be easy enough. I just need to take some measurements before I get started."

As Trakken got a measuring line from a nearby table and began to measure Victoria's wrists and gauntlets, Windmere joined the group outside. She set a leather pouch on another workbench and then beckoned Stephen over as she pulled out the pieces of the Kittrian sword that Stephen had accidentally shattered in his first battle.

"Are you going to try and fix my sword?" Stephen asked.

"I am going to do more than try. Hand me that tray, and I will set about fixing this and giving it some more durability as well," Windmere said with a smile.

Soon, the humans and Trodontians were all hard at work either making or repairing weapons.

After about thirty minutes had passed, Saralia brought them some breakfast before grabbing her longbow and leaving for another hunting trip, while the rest continued in their work.

After a few more hours of metalworking, the group heard a loud screech come from above them as Falamore and Vulant swooped down and landed outside.

"Ho, there! I see you are all hard at work!" Falamore said as he and his son entered the smithy.

"That we are, Falamore," Windmere said with a smile as she wiped the soot from her face. "Did you find any evidence of the gritters heading towards Altimi?"

"Unfortunately, we did. We found some sites where they had stopped for the night. From there, we found some tracks heading in the direction of Altimi," Vulant responded with a frown.

"Alright. See if you can find Clydesat and ask him if he and some of his warriors would be willing to accompany us to defend Altimi," Windmere requested as she returned to finishing Stephen's repaired sword.

"Aye, Windmere. We will be back within two hours and will be ready to depart from there," Falamore said as he and Vulant took off into the sky once more.

"Alright, Victoria, I think they are ready for you, now," Trakken said as he lifted up the newly-completed pair of Tekko-Kagi for her to try on. "I did make some changes to make them more suitable for combat, and you'll find that they aren't too heavy as well."

Victoria eagerly took the weapons and looked them over. The Tekko-Kagi had two blades jutting out about fourteen inches from her fingertips, which were protected by a piece of metal connecting both blades. They had leather straps fastened to them that were able to be tightened or loosened to accommodate the gauntlets or her wrists. The base of the blades fit neatly onto her forearm, nearly reaching her elbow. She tried strapping them on and found them to be a perfect fit. She tried a few practice swings and jabs with them, and, finding them to her satisfaction, she took them off and laid them on the table.

"Thanks for making these, Trakken! I will be sure to put them to good use," Victoria said as the blacksmith wiped the grease and soot from his hands on the apron.

Trakken smiled. "You are welcome, I do enjoy a challenging project, and yours was a good one to test my skills."

Stephen, meanwhile, was looking over his repaired sword and giving it a few practice swings.

"I'm really ready for those little pests now," he said with a grim smile.

"Good; we shall be facing them in a few days. I am going to get ready for the journey to Altimi; I would suggest you do the same," Windmere said as she walked back inside the house.

The next hour was a busy one, as the twins gathered what possessions they had with them, and, after wrapping their armor into bundles, they were soon ready to start. After they had finished preparing, Falamore and Vulant returned with Clydesat and the warriors who had agreed to come along.

Around high noon, the small army, numbering nearly two hundred warriors in all, made their way to the gates of Prariat, where they found a towering Trodontian waiting for them. Stephen looked at the fierce-looking warrior and leaned closer to Trakken.

"Who's that?"

"That is Galent, our chieftain," Trakken answered quietly.

Clydesat and Windmere approached Galent and gave the Trodontian salute, which the chieftain returned.

"I have heard of your mission, and I give you my blessing. May The One Above bring you victory and a safe return!" the chieftain said in a loud voice.

At this, the gate guards all drew their swords and held them high in the air. The warriors did the same, with the twins and Blakmians following suit. Soon, the army was trotting through the gate and out into the plains heading south.

As they were moving at a decent pace, Victoria spotted a flash of light from the top of a hill to her right. She turned on Windmere's back and looked over to see what could have made it when she saw Saralia dressed in shining armor, standing at the top of the hill, her long blond hair and horse tail blowing in the gentle breeze, while she watched the army pass below her.

Saralia then took off at a gallop down the hill and rushed over to Victoria and Windmere, her armor and weapons jingling as she kept pace with the rest of the army.

"I am coming with you," she said as she came alongside her mother and Victoria.

"Not this time. You are not ready to go into battle yet," Windmere said, grasping her daughter's hand as they trotted side by side.

"But I can fight."

"I know you can, but I also know that you aren't ready to enter pitched battle yet. You're still too young. Maybe, one day, you will have your chance, but I know that now is not the time for you to fight your first battle."

"Alright, you win. Just please be careful."

Saralia held out a leather pouch to Victoria, who took it and placed it into one of Windmere's saddlebags.

"Those are some healing herbs I gathered this morning. Use them when needed."

"Thank you. We will see you in a few days." Windmere said before she and Saralia gave each other a quick embrace before Saralia took off back up to the top of the hill and disappeared from view. Victoria heard Windmere sigh as she watched her daughter leave.

"She'll be fine, Windmere. She should be safe in your city," Victoria said, trying to reassure her friend.

"I know she will be. I am more concerned that I might not see her again. These battles keep getting bigger and the greatures and gritters more ferocious every time we clash. There may be a time where one of us won't come home."

Victoria slowly nodded in agreement and wondered what would happen if she or Stephen were hurt or killed here. What would their parents do without them? She thought about how their best friends Jack and Dani were supposed to come and visit in a few days. Would she and Stephen return the same time they left, or would their friends come, only to find them missing?

"No," she told herself. "It isn't good to worry about those things." They had a larger mission before them, and many lives were at stake. Even though this wasn't her world, she had fallen in love with it and its people, and she was determined to finish the job she and her brother had started and save this world. They were The Chosen Ones, after all; it was what they were supposed to do.

AFTER THEY HAD BEEN traveling all day at a decent pace, the army stopped for the night along the banks of a large river the twins were told was called the "Ice River," as the water was freezing cold.

As the army set up camp, Stephen looked around at his surroundings. There was a tall mountain range to their left, and the Ice River flowed in front of them, but from there, it turned south towards yet another range of mountains. In the distance, he could see what looked like a gap in the southern range, where the peaks were lower than the surrounding mountains.

"That must be where Altimi is," he said to himself when a voice spoke from behind him, making him jump in surprise.

"Aye, lad. Altimi is through that pass and behind the crossed path," Falamore said quietly. "We will arrive at the ruined portion of Altimi by noon tomorrow if we continue at this pace. But for now, lad, it is high time for some rest. We must be ready for the battle ahead."

Stephen nodded and walked over to the little tent Trakken had set up for him and crawled inside.

He was fast asleep and dreaming of becoming a legendary warrior when he woke up suddenly with a jolt. He had a sinking feeling something was wrong.

He sat up in the tent and looked around. The moonlight was shining in through the fabric of the tent, and he could see the shapes of the Trodontian army around him. He moved to the entrance of the tent and poked his head into the cold night air outside. He looked around but couldn't see anything.

He was about to go back into the tent when he caught sight of something out of the corner of his eye. He turned and could barely make out a silhouette dressed in dark blue with a hood covering its head moving silently through the camp. He was slightly over six feet tall and walked on two legs with its back towards him. He thought it might be one of their Blakmian companions but then he noticed he had a long furry tail like a cat's and no wings. He tried to get a closer look but slipped on the dewy grass and fell on his face. He quickly got up on his hands and knees and looked around but didn't see anything.

Guess I'm just seeing things, he thought to himself as he went back inside the tent and was soon asleep again.

VICTORIA WAS AWAKENED from her fitful sleep the next morning by a shout from Clydesat.

"Everyone, up! We march on Altimi today!"

Victoria quickly arose and was soon caught up in the bustle of the Trodontian army packing up their camp and getting ready to move on.

After a quick breakfast of porridge, the army was ready to move once more. The twins resumed their places on Windmere and Trakken's backs, and the army began its march southwards along the Ice River.

After an hour and a half, they reached a point where the river turned to the west once more; there, the army halted for a moment, as their scouts looked for a suitable place to cross the river. Stephen couldn't help but look up in amazement at what he saw. Only a few miles away, now, the southern range towered over them, and, wedged in between the mountains, he could see the crossed path. It was a tight roadway that made its way to the top of the ridge in a zigzag formation. There was also a tall waterfall that cascaded down the ridge and into the Ice River only fifty feet from the pathway. The deafening roar of the waterfall echoed around the mountain ranges and filled their ears as they approached.

Soon, the scouts found a good place for the army to cross the river. Victoria nearly shouted in surprise when the frigid water hit her legs but remained silent; her brother, on the other hand, did not.

"Wow! That water is cold!" he shouted.

Several of the nearby Trodontian soldiers snickered as they passed by, and a few more laughed at him.

"Why do you think it is called the 'Ice River?'" one of them jeered.

Stephen blushed and kept his mouth shut for the rest of the crossing.

After waiting for the rest of the army to join them on the other side, the army began the trek up the narrow, winding pathway up the side of the ridge. The path was so slim, only four warriors could walk side by side as they slowly began to climb up to the mountain pass.

After nearly an hour of climbing up the steep switchback pathway, with the roar of the waterfall constantly in their ears, they made it to the top. Stephen looked back down at the pathway from which they had come and saw to his horror that they were nearly a few hundred feet up from the banks of the Ice River. He turned away in fear and looked back at the pathway.

"That is right, lad. The important thing when high up is to not look down," Falamore chuckled as he and Vulant landed on the edge of the ridge.

"Why aren't you in the air?" Victoria asked the winged pair.

"They will probably see us coming and raise the alarm. We will walk with you for now," Vulant replied.

Victoria looked ahead and saw that the pathway was still a climb but was now a much gentler slope and going in a straight line in front of them. The river that fed the waterfall was only a few yards from the trail, flowing along the pathway. And much further ahead, she could see a tall stone wall that seemed to be ready to crumble away at any moment. Then, she noticed Clydesat motion for the soldiers to be quiet as they approached the ruined wall.

After another hour of slowly approaching the wall, the army gathered around it and hid behind it on both sides of the ruined gateway.

"What is your plan of attack, sir?" Clydesat asked Stephen.

"Do we know where the gritters are right now?" Stephen replied.

"I would wager that they would be hiding in the abandoned houses, waiting for nightfall to begin their attack, but I am not certain," Windmere said quietly.

Victoria spoke up: "I have an idea: why don't I climb the wall and try to find the gritters from there? Better yet, Stephen and I can try to force them out of their hiding places and make them come towards where you will be waiting."

"That sounds like a plan to me. Let's do it," Stephen said with a smile.

Clydesat silently agreed, and the twins got to work getting their armor on and making sure their weapons were secure. Then, they stood on Windmere and Trakken's shoulders and were just able to reach the top of the wall. The twins scrambled up, stood on the top of the wall, and looked at the ruined city, which lay before them. Hundreds of old stone houses, with thatched or wooden roofs, were rotting away everywhere they looked. The streets were roughly paved with cobblestones, and there was all manner of refuse lying around everywhere. Victoria couldn't help but notice that a lot of the houses didn't just have a front door, but they had wooden platforms with entryways on their roofs as well.

"I'll go right; you go left," Stephen whispered.

The twins began to make their way rooftop to rooftop, peering inside whenever possible, trying to find the gritters that they were almost certain would attack the city soon.

After a few minutes of jumping across the rooftops, the twins stopped when they heard the familiar screeching and grunting of the gritters. Stephen motioned for Victoria, who was a few houses away to his left, to stop and then pointed downwards into the ruined house he stood over. She nodded, looked into the house below her, then pulled her Tekko-Kagi from their holsters at her sides and jumped down into the house.

Immediately, a chorus of screeching ensued from within, and three gritters fled outside, followed closely by Victoria, her Tekko-Kagi claws already covered in the gritters' grey blood. Stephen looked down through the decaying thatched roof of his house and saw a sleeping greature directly below him and four gritters watching the chaos his sister was causing through the open doorway. He drew his sword and leaped down into the house, with his sword pointing downwards. He landed on the greature's shoulders and sank his sword into the beast's skull. The greature didn't even wake up as Stephen pulled his sword out of his victim's head and then turned to the small group of gritters that were nearby, as they turned around and stared at him in shock.

"Sorry, fellas! Hope you don't mind my dropping in!" he shouted as they turned and attacked. He quickly dealt with them and left the ruined house. He and his sister began to systematically go from building to building, driving the gritters from their hiding spots and into the roadways, where they came face to face with the Trodontian army, who was now charging down the streets and killing any gritter or greature that showed their faces.

After nearly fifteen minutes, Stephen was in the process of fighting another huge greature inside a larger house, when he heard a deafening roar come from outside. He quickly killed the beast, went outside, and looked down the street, only to see a large force of armored greatures and hundreds of gritters marching down the street towards him. Before he had a chance to react, a large wooden club came swinging around the corner of the house as he had to dodge an attack from another greature. Unfortunately, he wasn't fast enough, and the club caught him in the chest and knocked the wind out of him, sending him falling flat on his backside.

Stephen stared up at the large figure, who gave an evil smile and raised its club for another swing, when in a flurry of feathers and talons, he was attacked by Falamore from its right and Vulant from the left. The two slashed away with their razor-sharp talons, and, in moments, the beast lay dead.

Falamore held out his blood-soaked hand and helped Stephen to his feet. The three warriors looked at the oncoming army.

"Vulant, get to the city and try to get as much help as you can. I and the lad will stay here and try to keep them at bay as long as possible," Falamore said.

Vulant nodded and with a single flap of his wings took off into the sky, as Falamore looked at Stephen and managed a smile.

"Well, lad, you wanted a fight, did you not?! Ready yourself, as we are about to be in the thick of one!" he shouted as he also took off into the air, where he pulled out both of his longbows, one in his hands and the other in the grasp of his bird-like feet. He began to fire arrows as fast as he could into the approaching horde, while Stephen picked up both of his swords and got into a fighting stance, as the first few gritters picked up their pace and charged.

Stephen easily dealt with the first few gritters and then, with one of his blades, he blocked a large sword wielded by a greature that had come out of another house, and, with the other blade, he drove it deep into the monster's gut. Not a few seconds after the first one fell was another upon him that this one dropped to the ground before he could get to Stephen, an arrow lodged into its skull. A few seconds later, a third greature charged at Stephen, only for Victoria to leap from a nearby rooftop, land on his shoulder, and sink the blades of her Tekko-Kagi into his neck and then backflip off as he, too, fell to the ground.

"Having fun, Tori?!" Stephen shouted to Victoria over the noise of the battle as she stood by his side, her weapons raised for another attack.

"These things are awesome! I'm definitely keeping them!" she exclaimed as she slashed at a pair of gritters who had gotten too close for her liking.

Just then, the twins heard a noise rumbling like thunder on a summer evening, and they glanced behind them as they saw a force of Trodontians, led by Trakken, racing down the street towards them. The twins moved to the side to let the warriors pass, only for Trakken to grab Stephen and place him on his back, and another Trodontian warrior did the same with Victoria.

"Hold on tight!" Trakken shouted to the twins, as the Trodontian force raced towards the greatures and gritters, who had now picked up their pace and were now running at full speed towards their opponents. The Trodontians lowered their spears and pikes and, without slowing down, rammed into the greatures at full gallop, impaling many of them with their weapons as they smashed through the enemy line.

However, some were not as fortunate; out of the corner of his eye, Stephen watched the Trodontian warrior who had been making fun of him during the river crossing get swatted aside by a club wielded by a large greature. But before he could do anything to help, Stephen was already too far away, as he and Trakken continued their charge through enemy lines.

Within seconds, they and a few others had made it through the entire line, and they wheeled about, ready for a second charge, when they heard a large number of screeches coming from above them. Within moments, arrows began to rain down from the sky, and the enemy ranks began to drop like flies. Stephen looked up and couldn't help but cheer as he saw around twenty Blakmian archers led by Vulant soaring above them, cleaning up the remainder of the enemy forces around the city. Within minutes, the battle was over, and the rest of the Trodontian forces regrouped with their new Blakmian allies in what used to be an old marketplace.

"How many did we lose?" Stephen asked Clydesat when he saw the commander.

"Too many," came the grim reply. "They fought nobly and gave their lives for their friends and allies. We will never forget them."

The warriors took off their helmets with their heads bowed and gave the Trodontian salute, while the twins and Blakmians stood silently by. Stephen pulled off his helmet and thought of the warrior he watched in what may have been his final moments; he wished that he could have helped him somehow. He silently forgave the deceased warrior and looked back at the army, who were still quietly paying their respects for the fallen, when he noticed someone else was missing.

"Where's Falamore?" Stephen asked Victoria quietly.

"I don't know. He disappeared when Vulant showed up with reinforcements," she said in a whisper.

Suddenly, the silence was broken by a chorus of screams and screeches. The warriors looked up and saw hundreds of Blakmians flying overhead; however, they were not more warriors but women and children flying away from the city.

One young Blakmian woman flew towards the group and shouted at the warriors.

"Run away! The Shadowed One's army is attacking from the south! Altimi is falling!"

Chapter 9. Revelation and Requiem.

"Hurry! We must help defend Altimi!" Windmere cried out as the Blakmian warriors rocketed into the sky. Stephen got onto Trakken as the army took off at a gallop towards the city.

Victoria ran over to Windmere, who was already racing away at full speed. "Wait for me!" she shouted, but nobody could hear her over the thundering of hooves and the clatter of weapons.

Within moments, she was left alone in the ruined marketplace. She began to look around for anyone else who could give her a ride when she felt a pair of strong arms lift her off of the ground and into the air. She looked up and saw the grim face of Falamore as he lifted her onto his back, and he began to fly the two of them away from Altimi.

"Falamore! Thank goodness you're here! We need to help your people!"

"Lass, I told you I could go no further than the ruined city."

"I don't care! Your people need you! If you're looking to be a hero for them or something, now is the time to do it!"

Falamore soared in silence for a few moments as he watched the civilians flying away from their homes, carrying the weak and wounded in stretchers between them.

Suddenly, he turned around and began to fly towards the city.

"You may be right, lass. Perhaps it is time I return to my people," Falamore said with a determined look on his face. "We need to stop The Shadowed One's army here and now."

Victoria tightened her grip on her weapons as they flew towards the city in the sky. As they drew closer, she could see a large metropolis in the shape of a circle tucked neatly into the base of the surrounding mountains. As they flew, she could see thousands of Blakmians flying around: some trying to fly away, while others seemed to be exchanging blows and firing arrows against one other.

"By The One Above!" Falamore shouted. "The Shadowed One has turned my people against each other!"

The two of them flew close to some Blakmians, who were locked in combat with one other, but as soon as they saw Falamore and his rider, they stopped and looked at them, their jaws agape, before quickly flying away.

"That was strange," Victoria mused aloud to herself before feeling her stomach drop, as Falamore turned downwards and began to dive for a large building in the center of the city that seemed to be a palace.

"The brutes will be trying to take over the Palace of The Golden One. If we can kill their leader, we may be able to scare the rest of them away," Falamore said as he and Victoria sped down to a large balcony at the edge of the palace walls.

STEPHEN HELD ON FOR dear life as his Trodontian ride galloped at full speed towards the city gates, smashing any foe that got in their way with his war hammers. By the time they reached the gates, they could see that they were wide open, and there were gritters everywhere.

"Let's finish this fight once and for all!" Stephen shouted as they rapidly gained ground on their enemy.

Suddenly, arrows began to fall around them, and a few of the Trodontian warriors were hit and tumbled to the ground. Stephen and Trakken looked up in shock as they saw some Blakmian archers in the air firing at the approaching army.

"What are they doing?! We're trying to save their city, not attack it!" he yelled.

"They must be mercenaries in the pay of The Shadowed One!" Trakken shouted as he turned to the ruins of a large building that still had a roof and raced inside it for cover. A few other Trodontians also joined them inside just as a few arrows came through a hole in the roof and struck the earthen floor just in front of Trakken's forelegs, missing them by inches. Trakken reared back on his hind legs in surprise, causing Stephen to hit his head on the ceiling and fall off. Rubbing his head, Stephen jumped up and ran to the open doorway and watched as the Trodontian army searched to find cover from the barrage of arrows. To his horror, he saw those that were not able to find protection lying in the middle of the street.

Among those who lay dead or injured was Clydesat, his face frozen in a look of surprise and rage, with an arrow jutting out of his breastplate.

Stephen looked up and saw that their Blakmian attackers were now moving in to finish off the remainder of their forces. He ducked back behind the wall and closed his eyes, waiting for the sound of arrows hitting them when the noise of battle was split by a tremendous sound of a horn blasting from inside the city. The Blakmians stopped where they were, turned around in mid-air, and quickly took off towards the sound.

"Now's our chance!" Stephen shouted. He jumped up onto Trakken's back, and together, they and the other Trodontian forces began their attack once more, charging towards the city gates. Catching the gritters by surprise, they easily smashed through their lines. Soon, the Trodontian army was moving swiftly through the city streets, dodging burning houses, carts, and market stalls, killing any gritters or greatures they happened across. Stephen could hear countless screeches above him, and, from time to time, he would look up, only to see a whirling mass of feathers, arrows, and blades as Vulant and his company of Blakmians engaged the mercenaries that were in league with The Shadowed One.

However, it seemed like the mercenaries were getting the worst of it, as more and more Blakmians joined Vulant and pressed the assault on their traitorous comrades.

Another horn blast echoed through the city, and more Blakmians rose from the streets and the flocks of fleeing civilians and joined the swirling fight in the sky, while on the ground, Stephen, Trakken, and the Trodontian army pressed onwards towards the center of the city.

"What's our plan now?!" Stephen shouted over the constant noise of battle all around them.

"Head for the Palace of The Golden One! The leader of this dark army is most likely there! Once we kill him, the rest of his army will hopefully scatter and surrender!" Trakken shouted back.

Within ten minutes, the Trodontian army reached a large city square, and there, they could see the palace. It was a towering, white stone structure, with statues of former Blakmian rulers adorning its walls and worn-out banners hanging from the stained-glass windows. However, Stephen and the Trodontian army weren't concerned with what the palace looked like; it was the large group of well-armed and armored greatures as well as a few Blakmian fighters who stood in their way, spears and pikes lowered, ready for their attack. The Trodontian army halted at the edge of the square, unsure of what to do, when arrows began to rain down on the awaiting greatures, causing them to turn towards their attackers and raise their shields to protect themselves. A shout rang out from the sky above them.

"The king has returned! Protect the palace!"

Vulant and his enlarged company continued to shout with one voice as they continued to harass the greature army.

"Now! While they're distracted!" Stephen shouted as the Trodontian army resumed their charge towards the palace doors.

"For the King! For Lulandal!" the army roared in unison as they charged, their own spears and lances lowered and their swords and war hammers raised, ready to meet their enemy head-on.

FALAMORE LANDED ON the balcony, and Victoria jumped off of his back. Falamore quickly took off into the air once more.

"Go through the door at the edge of the wall and turn to your left; there, you will find the horn of the king. Two blasts of that should distract the traitors long enough for our friends to arrive at the palace. Once you have blown it two times, make your way to the throne room. If all goes well, I and our allies will meet you there," he said as he flew higher into the sky.

"What about you?!" Victoria called back as she tightened the straps on her Tekko-Kagi claws.

"There is something I must do to aid our allies on the ground. Now, go, lass! We do not have a moment to lose!" he shouted as he flew away at top speed.

Victoria didn't waste a second as she ran for the doorway at the edge of the balcony and, finding it locked, kicked it down. It fell onto the floor of a stone hallway, raising a large cloud of dust.

Before the dust cleared, she ran over the fallen door and slashed her way through the four gritters that had been standing guard. She sprinted down the hallway and slashed through any gritters who got in her way.

Soon, she came into a large, dusty room with a bronze tube, the end of which was wrapped in a dirty cloth sticking out of the wall to her left. She hurried over to the tube and saw an old piece of parchment tucked into the cover. She pulled it off and read its short message:

To be blown when the King returns.

"I don't know about a king returning, but here goes," she said to herself as she yanked the cover off, put her lips to the mouthpiece, and blew as hard as she could. A tremendous blast that shook the room came from the horn. Victoria leaned back to catch her breath when she felt a rough hand grasp her left arm.

She spun around, only to come face to face with the toothy grin of a greature. The greature laughed, its breath nearly causing her to gag.

"You have caused enough trouble for today. Time to die, you little pest," he hissed.

"I'd rather not, thanks," she said as she twisted her left arm and slashed at the beast's face with her right. The greature howled in pain and let go of her. She jumped back and raised her claws for another attack when the greature swung its right arm in a wide hook, managing to land a blow that sent her sprawling into the stone wall. Dazed from the first hit, she leaned against the wall, trying to gather her senses, when she saw a massive fist coming for her head. She tilted her head to the left, and the fist hit the stone wall, sending bits of rock flying. No sooner did the right fist pull back than the left fist came at her; she raised her right arm and blocked the punch, her Tekko-Kagi claws sinking deep into the beast's clenched hand. He roared in pain and staggered back, holding its left hand with its right, as its grey blood poured from its hand and face.

Victoria lunged at her attacker before he could get another blow in, sinking her claws deep into the monster's throat. She pulled her claws out of the monster's neck, and the greature gurgled, slumping to the floor with a thud. Victoria gasped for air after her duel and looked back to the mouthpiece of the horn.

"He did say blow it twice," she told herself as she took a deep breath once more, placed her mouth on the mouthpiece, and blew with all her might. The horn blast was nearly deafening at this point, and some of the old stones in the wall began to crack.

After exhausting her lungs on the horn, she fell onto the stone floor, still panting from her bout with the greature. She checked herself over and saw that while her armor was covered in the blood from the greature, and she had a few scratches from being knocked into the wall, but, other than that, she was fine.

She got up and walked out of the room and down the hallway, looking for a way to the throne room. As she walked, she could hear hoofbeats outside, and she ran to a nearby window and watched as the Trodontian army smashed into the greatures guarding the palace doors. She looked frantically for her brother and was relieved to see him riding Trakken; the two of them were in the process of striking down a greature when she heard another screech from her left. She turned and saw a gritter running at her; she quickly dealt with the annoyance, then looked back out the window and saw the Trodontian forces were making their way inside. She quickly began to follow the noise of the army below her and soon came to a large staircase. She jumped on the stone banister and slid down it and was nearly trampled by Trakken, who reared back in surprise.

"How did you get here so fast?!" Stephen shouted as he helped his sister get onto Trakken's back behind him.

"Falamore dropped me off on the palace wall. He said to meet him in the throne room," Victoria replied as Trakken took off at a gallop once more.

"And meet him we shall!" Trakken shouted as they rounded a corner and saw two huge golden doors. The army slid to a stop behind them, and Trakken walked over to the doors and pushed them open.

The doors slid open with a groan, and Trakken stepped inside. The twins looked in amazement at the room they found themselves in. It was like the chapel of a cathedral with a very high vaulted ceiling made of reddish wood. The walls and floor were made from a stone that looked like white marble; the light of the setting sun shone through large stained-glass windows along the walls with images depicting scenes from Blakmian history. However, one of the windows had been broken, and its colorful pieces were scattered across the floor.

Against the back wall was a large golden throne that seemed to be decorated with golden feathers, but in front of this throne stood a creature that the twins had never seen before. He was a tall, menacing figure that was nearly nine feet in height. He had dark, stone-like skin, and his eyes were a bright blue, nearly glowing in the daylight. He was wearing a set of black, ebony-like armor, wielding a mace the size of a truck tire in his right hand and wearing a large spiky gauntlet on his left hand.

Trakken let out a gasp when he saw the enemy warrior in front of them.

"An Unkarian?! I thought they were dead or locked up after the great war!" he shouted across the room.

The beast laughed, a great booming laugh, and spoke: "You will wish that were true! We have suffered under the Black Peak for long enough! We have come to claim what is rightfully ours!"

Stephen and Victoria jumped to the ground and raised their weapons.

"The Shadowed One, I presume?" Stephen asked confidently.

"You are wrong, little warrior. I am Thaliton, second in command under my lord The Shadowed One," the warrior responded with a sneer. "However, if you would like to meet my master, you need to only look behind you."

Stephen felt something wet hit his helmet, and he looked up and immediately froze in fear, his mouth open in a silent scream. Victoria, seeing her brother go as white as sheet, looked up and to see what had made her brother lock up, and she saw something that nearly made her faint in sheer terror.

Hanging on the wall behind them just above the doorway was a colossal black spider over twenty feet across. Its eight legs clung to the sides of the room, and its eight glowing red eyes were gazing hungrily at the twins and their companions, saliva dripping from its mouth. On the spider's back was another Unkarian, even taller than the first at nearly ten feet in height. His muscular body was covered in a gleaming set of grey plate armor, and he wielded a huge, seven-foot-long curved sword and a massive shield the size of a dinner table.

The warrior jumped off his mount's back and landed in front of the twins, the floor shaking when he landed. The huge spider crawled across the wall and out of the shattered window.

"You must be two of The Chosen Ones the story tells of," the massive warrior said with an evil smile.

Stephen finally managed to snap out of his trance and turn back to face their opponent.

"Yes, we are! W-we are here to defeat you and bring peace to the land!" Stephen shouted, his voice still a little shaky.

The Shadowed One and Thaliton both laughed at the two of them.

"You have little chance without the true Chosen One! You have no hope of defeating me without him, and even if he was here, I would still win!"

"We're not just some kids who were given weapons and told to fight a war! We can beat you and your entire army right here, right now!" Stephen shouted as he raised his two swords and took a step closer towards their giant foe, who laughed once more.

"If it is defeat you want, I will not hold back from giving it to you!" The Shadowed One snapped his fingers, and suddenly, all of the windows around them were smashed, and dozens of hulking greatures and hundreds of gritters poured in through the broken glass. Soon, the twins and their Trodontian and Blakmian comrades were surrounded.

"You see? You have no hope of winning this fight on your own," The Shadowed One said. As he turned around and stepped away from the twins, he whispered, "Admit it: you're too weak."

Stephen's face went red with rage, and before Victoria could stop him, he lunged at the dark king and swung his swords at his back. The monster spun around quickly and swung his shield at Stephen, who ducked under it and jumped up, only to have to raise his swords to block another attack, this time from the monster's huge sword. The massive sword collided with the point of Stephen's repaired Kittrian blade, but instead of stopping or being deflected away, the huge sword cut into it, its blade sinking halfway down towards the hilt. Stephen looked at it in shock as the Shadowed One twisted the sword out of his hand and, before Stephen could react, swung his shield again; this time, Stephen caught the full force of the blow and was sent flying into the stone wall. Stephen tried to push himself up but fell on his face, unconscious.

"Your blades may have been forged by the best blacksmiths in the land, but only one blade can stand against the ancient might of The Ruler's Sword, and you cannot wield it!" The Shadowed One said mockingly as he turned to Stephen's unconscious form.

Victoria watched as the giant stepped closer to her brother's still body and raised a massive fist, ready to crush her brother with a single blow. She raced over to her brother and stood over him, her Tekko-Kagi claws raised, as the huge fist came down. She felt her claws sink into the huge hand, and the Shadowed One grunted in surprise, lifted his hand up, and looked at the wound. To Victoria's horror, the wound was healing itself at a rapid rate; soon, only a small scar was in its place.

"You should have learned more about Unkarians. We can heal our wounds faster than you can inflict them. You stand no chance with those little pieces of scrap metal," The Shadowed One said with a sneer.

'We'll see about that!" Victoria screamed as she rushed at the massive warrior. She darted around the giant's huge legs and slashed wherever she could find an opening, all the while dodging attacks from his sword and shield. Suddenly, she heard a huge crash to her left, and she stopped for a second to see the massive sword falling to the ground.

"Tori! Watch out!" she heard her brother shout, but it was too late, as a massive hand grabbed her left arm and squeezed. She screamed in pain as she felt her shoulder come out of its socket. The Shadowed One tossed her to where her brother was just struggling to his feet. They collided into each other with a clattering of metal and a cry of pain from Victoria as she landed on her injured shoulder.

The Shadowed One turned to the Trodontians, who were standing nearby.

"You see them? Do you see what your 'Chosen Ones' can do? They cannot help you! Nobody can!" he said mockingly. "And now, I will end their pathetic lives before I end yours!"

He raised his huge sword, ready to strike the finishing blow when a loud voice thundered through the doorway and an arrow struck his helmet, glanced off, and embedded itself into the throne, causing the Shadowed One to look up from his two battered victims.

"I say to thee, nay!"

The Trodontian army stepped aside as a Blakmian clad in gleaming golden armor strode into the throne room, his longbow drawn with an arrow at the ready.

"Halt there, foul brigand! By the order of Falamore! Son of the Golden King! The rightful heir to the throne of Altimi!" Falamore shouted as he placed another arrow on his bowstring.

"So, you have returned after all? Well, you're just in time to watch your city burn and your people run away in terror," the monster sneered.

"Not this day! Not ever!" Falamore bellowed. "I challenge you to a king's duel! The victor takes the city. The defeated shall take their army and leave!"

"If that is how you want it, I accept," the dark king said with a grim smile.

The greatures spread out, forming an open circle for the two combatants. Stephen and Victoria staggered to their feet and felt a taloned hand on their shoulders.

"We need to leave," Vulant whispered. "My father will keep them distracted long enough for us to escape. He will join us on the outside of the city later."

Stephen nodded and began to follow Vulant through the crowd of greatures. Victoria looked on as Falamore took off into the sky and began to fire arrows at the monster who raised his shield, trying to protect himself. A few arrows found their mark in the Shadowed One's shoulders and legs.

The beast roared in frustration. "Enough of this! Time to bring you to my level!" he shouted as he dropped his shield.

Victoria noticed that the shield had two chains attached to it instead of handles. The chains went from the back of the shield and wrapped around the Shadowed One's left arm. The Shadowed One began to swing his shield around his head like a flail, and, to Victoria's horror, she watched as the side of it caught Falamore in midair, snapping his bow and breaking one of his wings. Falamore screamed in pain as he fell to the ground and landed in a crumpled heap.

The Shadowed One stepped over Falamore and grinned.

"I have won. Surrender the city, and I may let you live," the Shadowed One said with a twisted smile.

Falamore struggled to his feet, his face battered and his left wing hanging loosely behind him, but there was a fire in his eyes and defiance on his face.

"Not while I draw breath," he said grimly as he drew his two short swords and pounced at his opponent, screaming, "Have at thee!"

Victoria tried to move closer to the dueling kings but felt herself being pulled back towards the doorway by Trakken.

"We need to leave, now," he whispered in her ear as she tried to pull away from his strong grasp.

"We have to help Falamore!" she pleaded.

"He is buying us time to escape," Trakken said as he picked her up, put her on his back, and began to walk away from the fight.

As they left the throne room, Victoria looked back and saw Falamore and The Shadowed One were locked in combat, with metal clashing against metal, but it was clear that Falamore was having the worst of it. His helmet had been knocked off and subsequently crushed. One of his swords had been broken in two, while the other had been completely shattered; nevertheless, Falamore kept on the attack, slashing away at any weak point in the giant's armor with the talons on his hands and feet. Victoria got a sick feeling in her stomach as she turned to face Stephen and the rest of the remaining Trodontian army.

"He's not going to win that fight," Victoria said, her eyes beginning to water from the pain in her body and her sadness as she realized that her friend who had saved her several times was now saving her and her brother one last time.

"He knows," Vulant said quietly. "His plan is to buy us time to escape and regroup."

"Then, let us fall back to the city gates before the enemy decides to stop being chivalrous," Trakken said as he and the Trodontians began to hurry out of the palace.

As they moved along the main hallway, the greatures and gritters stood aside and let them by. A few Blakmians stood by and glared at them as they passed, but the twins ignored them. Just as they reached the main door, they heard a triumphant roar echo down the hallway, and when the greatures and gritters heard it, they lifted their heads and echoed the sound. Stephen and most of the Trodontians bowed their heads, and a few of them gave a quick salute. Victoria began to cry softly to herself as the defeated army made their way across the palace square, now illuminated by moonlight.

Suddenly, they heard a loud screech coming from behind them, and when they looked back, they saw a huge swarm of gritters pouring out of the palace like a river of claws and teeth.

"Run!" Trakken shouted before breaking into a gallop. Stephen and Victoria held on tightly as they sped away from the palace and out of the city. Soon, they were in the ruined side of the city once more, and as they reached the old gate, they slowed down.

Suddenly, a familiar figure limped out of the shadow of a house and into the moonlit roadway, causing the army to come skidding to a halt. Stephen was in shock at whom he saw: it was Windmere, but she was in very bad shape; her helmet was gone, and the rest of her armor was dented or missing. She had numerous cuts and scratches covering her face, arms, and flanks; a few arrows were sticking out of her horse half, and her right foreleg was covered in blood and held aloft as she limped on her three good legs.

"Mother!" Trakken shouted as he hurried over to her. "Thank The One Above you are alive!"

Windmere coughed and managed a weak smile. "I was swarmed by gritters and some of those traitorous Blakmians, while I was trying to take cover in an alleyway."

"Can you make it outside the city?" Trakken asked as he walked over to her and gave her his shoulder for support.

"I could make it back to Prariat on one good leg. I will be fine," she said with a weak chuckle. "I have been through worse."

The warriors slowly made their way out of the ruined city, Trakken trying to help his mother walk along the stony ground.

As they left the city, they heard a voice from behind them.

"Halt!"

Stephen turned around and saw three figures behind them, two of which were greatures who carried a stretcher between them; the third one was a much more lean figure that seemed to walk on its tiptoes, dressed in dark blue clothes that seemed to melt into the night sky. Its face was mostly covered, save for its bright green eyes that glowed in the darkness. Stephen also saw that the figure had a long, cat-like tail covered in bluish-gray fur, tipped with a dark metallic point. The greatures silently walked over to the Trodontian army, as Vulant and his remaining Blakmian allies landed in a circle around them, their weapons drawn.

Vulant took one look at the stretcher and let out a cry of grief and turned away sobbing. Victoria slid off Trakken's back and, ignoring the searing pain in her shoulder, walked closer to the stretcher. She couldn't help but start crying once she saw the thing she dreaded most.

On the stretcher was Falamore's lifeless body, battered and bloody, his golden armor crushed, his broken wings wrapped around him. His face, however, despite the bruises and specks of blood, seemed peaceful and content as if he somehow knew that he had fulfilled his purpose and saved his friends one last time. Stephen and the rest of the army pulled off their helmets and bowed their heads in respect for their fallen friend.

The cat-like figure silently stepped forward and spoke in a smooth, monotone voice.

"The Shadowed One sends his regards for your fallen comrade. He fought with honor and nobility. He sends you his body to bury in your own fashion, and, in his mercy, he is giving you twenty hours to cross the Ice River and leave his territory. Those who are still here after the twenty hours have passed will live to regret their foolish decision."

Windmere limped forward towards the figure, her face a look of sadness and confusion.

"Ripper? Is that you?" she quietly asked.

The figure responded by throwing two small knives into the necks of the greatures who had dropped the stretcher and who were still standing nearby, their lifeless bodies falling to the ground with a soft thump. He then pulled down his hood and mask, revealing a feline face with grey fur and cat-like ears.

"It is I. The Shadowed One wanted me to scare you off and dump the body in the river. I, however, cannot bring myself to do that. Falamore was an ally when we served together against the pirates of the coast. I brought his body to you so you can give him the funeral the noble warrior deserves," the cat-like assassin said quietly.

"Why are you working with that evil Unkarian?!" Windmere shouted.

"Because they will destroy my village and slaughter my family if I do not," the assassin said as he turned his back to the army.

"You know that he will most likely betray you," Trakken countered.

"He would not," the assassin said as he pulled up his mask and hood once more. "I would kill him first." He then jumped up on top of the stone wall and vanished into the shadows.

The army stood there in silence for a few moments before Vulant spoke up, his voice still quivering from his tears.

"We must give my father, the king, a proper funeral ceremony."

The Blakmians silently nodded and got to work.

Soon, they had found an old boat by the riverside and pulled it ashore, while Trakken saw to his mother's and Victoria's injuries, using the herbs his sister had given them. The Blakmians then built a funeral pyre on the boat and laid their fallen king, his body covered by his great wings, on top of it. Shortly after, the boat was floating in the

MIDDLE OF THE RIVER, held back from floating away by a rope that Vulant was holding while he stood on the riverbank.

A number of Blakmian and Trodontian archers, including Windmere, stood by with flaming arrows on their bowstrings. The rest of the army stood with Stephen and Victoria along the river in silence.

Vulant held up one hand and bowed his head with his eyes closed, tears still running down his face.

"May The One Above greet you in the sky while we cry in mourning, for a great king has fallen...a great king who was a father to me, a friend to many, and a champion of thousands. Falamore, my father, may you have safe travels to the realm above, and may we see you again one day."

Vulant then let go of the rope and watched as the river's current began to take the boat away. The archers then raised their bows and launched their flaming arrows at the boat, many of which struck the pyre and set it ablaze. The Blakmians folded their wings and bowed their heads, while the Trodontian army gave their own salute with their faces towards their fallen comrade.

Victoria looked over at her brother, her eyes still watering, and could see her brother, who always liked to be seen as the big, tough older sibling, was crying too.

"I want to go home," she said quietly as she reached out and grasped his hand in hers, and they stood side by side, watching the pyre slowly float away.

"Me too," he whispered. "I thought this would be a fun adventure, a time where we could be the heroes and save the world, but now...." His voice trailed off into quiet crying once more.

The whole company watched in silence as the flaming boat drifted down the river towards the waterfall until it came to the top, where it seemed to hesitate for a moment before plunging downwards and disappearing from view. The army stood quietly for a few minutes until Windmere's voice broke through the silence.

"Falamore was a good friend and ally whenever I needed him. He was always willing to help those who needed it most. And he proved that once more to us today. May we never forget his sacrifice and not make it useless. We will regroup back at Prariat and figure out what we will do from there."

The army quietly nodded, picked up their gear, and began making their way down the crossed path in silence. Stephen and Victoria quietly walked beside each other, wondering what they would do now.

Chapter 10. Learning and Loss.

After making their way slowly down the crossed path and across the Ice River, the defeated army encamped on the opposite bank.

Stephen climbed into his tent and was soon asleep. Victoria laid on her sleeping mat, but blessed slumber refused to come to her. She kept seeing the events she had witnessed that day: The Shadowed One on his huge spider steed hanging on the wall behind them; her brother and herself getting brutally beaten; Falamore's broken body lying on the ground; the funeral for the fallen king; even the numerous greatures and gritters she had killed.

She rolled over on her left side and felt a sharp pain in her shoulder. She sat up quickly and rubbed the sore joint.

"I'd better be more careful with that," she told herself quietly. She then heard the noise of heavy footfalls near her tent. She looked over, and, through the fabric of the tent walls, she could see the shadow of a Trodontian limping past her.

"Windmere? Is that you?" she whispered.

The shadow stopped and turned slightly towards the tent.

"Yes, child. Go back to sleep." Windmere whispered back before continuing to limp towards the river.

Victoria hesitated for a few seconds before wrapping herself in a thick blanket and leaving her tent to follow Windmere to the edge of the river. Windmere slowly walked into the water and gingerly lowered her injured leg into the icy river. She winced when the cold water lapped at her injuries but held her leg there.

"I told you to go back to sleep," Windmere said to Victoria without even turning around.

"I can't sleep," Victoria said sadly as she sat down in the grass. Windmere let out a deep sigh.

"Nor can I. This has been one of the hardest days in my life. Only the day I lost my husband was worse than this one."

"How did he die?"

Windmere stepped back from the water and slowly laid down in the grass next to Victoria.

"He was killed by raiders over fifteen years ago. I was expecting my little Saralia when I got the news of his death."

"I'm sorry. That must have been horrible."

"I was ready to end it all for a few days after I learned of my dear Halep dying. But I did not...because Falamore was there to encourage me. His friendship helped me through that dark time. And now...."

Windmere's voice trailed off as her eyes began to well up with tears. Victoria slid up to her friend and leaned against her.

"He was a good friend to me, too. I know we'll all miss him."

Windmere looked down at Victoria and managed a weak smile before a concerned look came over her face.

"Are you alright?"

"I keep thinking about what I have been doing while I have been here. I've...I've been killing dozens of living creatures, fighting in real battles...it's all just sinking in, now. That beating I got from The Shadowed One brought me back to reality. I'm nothing more than a murderer!"

Victoria stood up and turned away from Windmere. She started to walk away but felt a hand on her shoulder.

"I know how you feel. War is never a pleasant thing to go through for most people. I wish our land was peaceful, but I know that is far from the case. In this world, sometimes it is kill or be killed. Killing is something every warrior has to come to terms with. Not everybody likes to take another life, even if those you are fighting are little more than animals, like the gritters."

Victoria walked back to Windmere's side and laid down against her warm horse body. She looked up at the sky and watched the clouds slowly move overhead and sighed.

"It's just a lot to take in. My brother and I trained to sword fight, and I trained for hand-to-hand combat because I wanted to. I didn't want to have to use my skills against another living being. But I just got caught up in the excitement of being in a different world and becoming a part of something bigger, like being one of The Chosen Ones. I felt like I could take on everything that came my way. But I can see tonight I was wrong...and now, a good friend has paid the price."

Windmere pulled Victoria into a motherly embrace and held her close, both with tears running down their faces.

"I know it seems like we cannot win now, but sometimes, things have to get worse before they can get better. We have to try to defeat that monster before he destroys everything we hold dear."

The two warriors sat together in silence for a few minutes before Victoria spoke up again.

"Windmere, who's Ripper? You made it sound like you knew him when he brought back Falamore."

Windmere let out a deep sigh and stretched her forelegs out in front of her.

"Firstly, Ripper is not his real name. It is actually Bomski. He prefers 'Ripper,' as it makes him sound more intimidating. He is an Amronian mercenary who lives in the village of Felinad."

"When I was a young warrior, Halep, Falamore, Ripper, and I would wander the coast, visiting towns and aiding them against raiders and the occasional greature attack. After a while, we began to notice Ripper beginning to enjoy his work too much, and when we talked to him about it, he got upset and vanished. I have not seen him since, but I had heard reports of him showing up from time to time, normally doing a quick job and disappearing again. He is a formidable fighter and enjoys playing with his targets. I heard he will scratch an 'x' shape in a tree or something near his target before he either kills them or captures them."

"But enough of that. We both need to try and get some sleep."

Windmere slowly stood up and began to limp away, leading Victoria back to her tent. Before Windmere walked away, Victoria grabbed her hand and held her back.

"I think we need to let Groman know what happened. Could we try and send a message to him to meet us at Prariat?"

Windmere silently nodded and limped away. Victoria climbed back inside her tent, laid down on her sleeping mat once more, and, this time, she was soon asleep.

THE TRIP BACK TO PRARIAT was slow but uneventful, with the army nearing the city walls by sunset.

Victoria was walking by Windmere's side, while Stephen rode on Trakken's back. Neither of the twins spoke very much during the journey; they had many things on their minds, but neither of them knew quite what to say.

Their trains of thought were broken when a shout came from the city gates.

"Mother!"

Victoria and Windmere looked up as Saralia galloped over to them and slid to a halt. Mother and daughter embraced, and Saralia looked over her mother's injuries.

"Thank The One Above you are alive! Come with me. I have some medicine and bandages waiting for you. And do not argue with me!"

They began to walk away when Saralia looked back at Victoria, Stephen, and Trakken.

"Chieftain Galent, Elder Gilder, and Groman are waiting for you in the great hall," Saralia said. "I shall be there as soon as I can get Mother fixed up and resting."

Trakken nodded, and the trio made their way to the great hall. It was a large wooden structure with one huge meeting room inside. The room had a dirt floor and to the sides were a few desks and map tables. The whole room was lit by oil lamps and a large hearth at the far side of the room. In the center of the hall stood Chieftain Galent and two Kittrians whom the twins recognized as Groman, his massive sword still on his back, and Elder Gilder of Areiop. The three men turned to face Trakken and the twins when they entered.

Galent stepped forward towards the trio before he spoke.

"What happened, Trakken? We heard of your loss and the deaths of many of our warriors, including my nephew Clydesat, but we do not know what caused it."

Trakken took a deep breath as Stephen jumped off of his back and joined his sister on the ground.

"*He* was there. The Shadowed One invaded Altimi from the south, as we pressed our attack from the north. We were caught by Blakmian mercenaries under his control, and they were the ones who killed so many of our soldiers. However, we pressed on to the palace, where we saw him for the first time and learned of his true nature and power. The Shadowed One is an Unkarian wielding the Ruler's Sword. He commands an army like we have never seen since the Great War, and he has become too powerful for even Stephen and Victoria."

The two leaders looked at each other in shock and disbelief, while Groman began to turn white.

"This is bad news indeed," Elder Gilder said with a look of worry on his face.

"We will discuss what our next course of action is to be," Galent said as he and the elder walked out of the room.

Groman walked over to the twins, his face turning as white as a sheet of paper.

"Is he really here?" Groman asked quietly.

Stephen's face turned red, and he stared at Groman. "What do you mean, 'Is he really here?' He not only beat me and broke my sword as if it was a twig, but he crushed Victoria and killed Falamore! If that isn't a good indication that this whole land is in danger, I don't know what is!"

"I understand! You want me to do something about it! But I already told you I will not fight!" Groman shouted back.

"Then give me your sword. He said only one warrior could stand against him wielding The Ruler's Sword, and I bet it's yours," Stephen said coldly.

"Stephen!" Victoria whispered in shock.

"You want it? Come and take it," Groman said, walking over to a table, unstrapping The Empty Sword, and laying it down before walking to the side of the room.

Stephen walked over to the weapon and reached out for the sword's handle. But when he grabbed it, he felt something like a strong electrical current shock his outstretched palm and fingers, and he jumped back in surprise, rubbing his hand.

"What was that?!" he shouted in pain as Groman walked back to his sword and easily picked it up, strapping it to his back again.

"Only I can wield this weapon. That is how they knew I was The Chosen One. They would bring the sword to the Kittrian villages, and the people would try to see if they could grasp its hilt without getting injured. It is only a burden to me and dead weight. But as I am The Chosen One, I am bound to this weapon, and I must carry it wherever I go."

"I'm sorry, Groman. I didn't know," Stephen said quietly. "But we do need your help. If you don't fight, who knows what that monster will do next."

The four warriors stood there quietly when they heard a chorus of peeping and chirping coming from above them. They looked up and saw two flying lizards, one emerald green and the other a dark blue, had flown in through a window and were coming towards them.

"Oh, no. Not these again," Stephen said as he ducked behind Trakken's horse half, but to his annoyance, the lizards flew over to him and landed on his left arm and head. "Come on! Why me?" he moaned as Victoria and Trakken grabbed the messages off the lizards' tails.

As they read the messages, their faces grew pale, and looks of shock and horror came over them as they exchanged papers and read the other's message.

"What's wrong?" asked Stephen as he tried to shake the lizards off, but they seemed content where they were.

Trakken took both messages and handed them to Groman, who also turned pale when he read them.

"Two villages to the south have been captured, and their peoples have been taken as prisoners," Victoria said in a grave tone. "That makes three cities lost to The Shadowed One in just over twenty-four hours."

Groman crumpled the papers in his hand and walked over to a map table. The others followed, with Stephen still trying to shake his lizard passengers off.

Groman pointed to two cities on the map. "These are the two that have been taken today. It would seem that The Shadowed One is making a push towards either the coastline or up into the Kittrian forest."

"What do you think he's planning?" Victoria asked before being interrupted by the chirping of another lizard—this time, a bright red one—flying down towards the group. Stephen ducked, and his two passengers jumped off him and flew away. Groman held out his arm, and the lizard flew over to it and landed on his outstretched hand. The lizard held its head up. Groman scratched it under its chin, and the lizard closed its eyes and began to purr.

"Hello, my Little Flyer. Do you bring me a letter from my sister again?" Groman asked as he gently plucked the paper off of its tail, and the lizard then climbed onto his shoulder and seemed to fall asleep, while Groman read the message in silence.

When he finished the letter, his face became red, and he threw it onto the table and stormed over to the middle of the open room before falling to his knees and holding his head in his hands.

Victoria grabbed the paper and looked at the message:

Dear Brother,

Somehow, the elder found out about my helping Tori and Steve, and I will probably be captured soon. As much as I want you to come and rescue me, I know you have a mission more important than me, and I do not want to distract you from it. Do not worry about me. I will be fine. You must go and save the world and make our parents proud! And I will be awaiting your victorious return!

Your loving little sister,

Annalio.

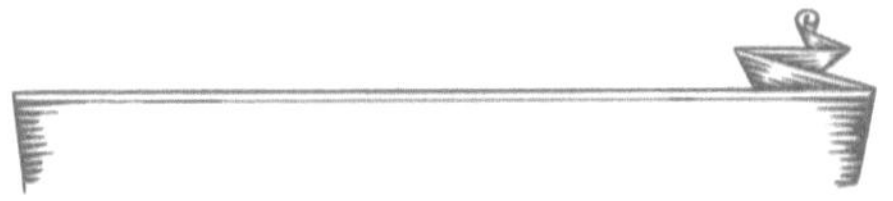

Chapter 11. Recon and Rescue.

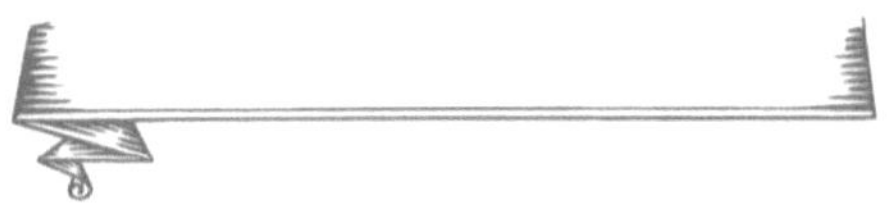

"No...." Victoria's voice quivered as she dropped the letter on the table. Her hands began to shake. Groman was on his knees in the middle of the great hall, softly crying to himself. Stephen and Trakken stood by in silence.

Then, Saralia walked into the room and surveyed the scene before walking over to the map table, and, upon seeing and reading the three depressing letters, she stepped backward in shock.

"What are we going to do?" asked Victoria quietly.

Groman stood up from where he was kneeling and walked over to the group, his face becoming red with rage.

"I will tell you what I am going to do! I am going to get my little sister from those thugs!" he said as he started to leave the room, only to be stopped by Steve and Trakken.

"Not alone, you're not. You'll only be walking to your death if you go alone. Besides, Annie has most likely been taken away by now, so going back to your home village won't be of any use besides dealing with that traitor of an elder," Stephen said firmly.

"But we are going to do something, right?" Groman pleaded. "I cannot live knowing my little sister is in their clutches. She...she is all I have left."

"We *are* going to do something!" Saralia said, stomping a hoof on the dirt floor. "I suggest we travel down to those villages and try to save as many people as we can, as well as trying to find out The Shadowed One's master plan. I am guessing he has been playing you this whole time and is counting on your defeat at Altimi to slow your reaction to the other villages being captured. It is time we find out what our enemies are up to and beat them at their own game!"

The others nodded in agreement, except for Victoria, who looked at Saralia in concern.

"What about your mother? I thought she didn't want you to go into battle."

"Mother is too injured to fight again for a while; besides, I may have slipped her some sleeping herbs while I took care of her wounds. She will be asleep for at least a day or two. And I said we would be scouting ahead and trying to get information about The Shadowed One's next move. We are not planning to go into battle at all, right?" Saralia said with a sly grin.

"I see. Well, when do we leave?" Victoria asked.

"At sunrise tomorrow. I have already gathered some supplies for the journey ahead. You and I can head to Jeatut, while the boys go to Gadwar."

"Sounds like a plan to me. But we should try to stay out of trouble; nobody is ready for a big battle again," Trakken said.

"Well, Groman? Are you coming with us?" Stephen asked as he looked over at their Kittrian companion.

"I am willing to go, as long as we are not planning to fight," Groman replied.

"I would still highly recommend you bring your weapons anyways…just in case," Saralia said. "Now, we all need to get some sleep before our journey tomorrow."

The group left the great hall and made their way back to Windmere's house, where they went to bed and were soon asleep.

VICTORIA WAS AWAKENED the next morning by Saralia gently shaking her shoulder.

"Time to go!" Saralia whispered excitedly in Victoria's ear.

Victoria swung out of her hammock and hurried into the main room, where she found Trakken, Stephen, and Groman eating breakfast. Saralia had left her a bowl of oatmeal with some berries on the table for her, and Victoria quickly sat down and soon had it finished.

Once the group was ready, they made their way into the enclosed smithy and made sure their weapons were sharpened and ready for battle. Stephen left his broken Kittrian blade on a workbench and picked up a shield instead. Trakken left his war hammers and instead grabbed a large two-handed broadsword and a mace. Saralia fastened her two scimitars to her sides and equipped her longbow and a quiver full of arrows, all while Victoria sharpened her Tekko-Kagi claws, and Groman stood nearby, polishing The Empty Sword.

Soon, the group was on their way to the main gate, and they momentarily found themselves walking across the open plains.

"Here is where we split and go to our separate targets. Good luck to you, boys. I hope you find your sister, Groman," Saralia said as she helped Victoria onto her back.

Groman nodded, and he and Stephen climbed aboard Trakken and, with a wave, took off southwards. Saralia and Victoria turned to the west and were soon trotting at a good clip across the grassy fields.

After a few hours, they stopped at a small stream, where they refilled their flasks and rested for a while.

"How long will it take to get there, Saralia?" Victoria asked.

"Over a day at least. We need to cross the entirety of the shadowed plains."

"Have you been to Jeatut before?"

"Well, I have been there once or twice to trade some furs and meat, but I never went alone; Mother was always with me. But I know the area around it quite well, though. It is mostly forest, but it is not too thick, and it is good hunting ground."

After chatting for a few minutes, the two of them got up and took off again into the late morning air.

They traveled on for the rest of the day before they stopped by a small grove of trees for the night. Saralia went hunting with her bow and soon brought back an animal that looked and tasted like a deer, but it had three horns jutting from its head and two long tails.

After a delicious dinner of meat cooked over an open fire, the two warriors went to sleep under a clear, starry sky.

The next morning, they set off again after a quick breakfast and continued their trek across the shadowed plains.

In the late afternoon, they reached the edge of a large forest. The trees almost seemed to cast a sinister shadow below them, and Victoria could barely see another mountain range to the south that rose like sharp teeth into the sky. The mountain range seemed to slice into the southern side of the woods. The grey and brown stone stood out among the dark green trees.

"Well, we are only a few miles away from the forest, now, and that would mean we are about ten miles from Jeatut. Have you thought about what we are going to do when we get there?" Saralia asked.

"I'll try to have an idea when we get closer."

The two approached the forest and were soon enveloped by the trees. Saralia began to act a bit nervous and nearly reared back on her hind legs in surprise when they came upon an old skeleton of a gritter lying against a tree.

"What's wrong, Sara?"

"Can you not hear it?"

"I don't hear anything."

"Exactly! There would normally be the sound of all of the woodland creatures like Hillus, Grelout, and Nut-snatchers. This...this is just silence aside from the wind in the trees."

"That could mean there is a hunter nearby. And I doubt it's us. How close are we to the village?"

"Another mile, I think."

"Let me get off, now. We should try to sneak up on them from here."

Saralia stopped, and Victoria slid off her back and pulled her Tekko-Kagi claws from their sheaths. Together, they quietly made their way through the woods.

Suddenly, Saralia halted and held her hand out to stop Victoria. Saralia slowly pointed to something ahead of them, and Victoria peered into the darkness and saw a large wooden wall not fifty feet ahead of them. But in front of that wall stood two gritters who hadn't seen them yet, their grey bodies lit up by the moonlight.

"Stay in the shadows. We do not want to raise the alarm," Saralia whispered as she drew her longbow.

"Think you can take them out with your bow?"

"Easily," the huntress replied with a grim smile as she laid an arrow on the string. "The trick is to get one when the other is not looking, so they do not know what happened."

"Leave that to me," Victoria said as she crouched low and began to slowly creep through the underbrush.

After crawling for a few minutes, she found herself behind a fallen tree and poked her head out to look at her targets. The two gritters were looking into the forest in Saralia's general direction, but neither of them had been detected yet. When Victoria looked closer, she could just barely make out the outline of Saralia's light brown horse half hidden in the shadow of a huge tree. She picked up a large piece of rotten wood and tossed it a few feet to her right. The piece of wood rustled the plants, and one of the gritters quickly hurried over to where the noise had come from. Victoria watched the other gritter get pinned to the wall by an arrow, and before the other gritter knew what happened, he met the same fate.

Victoria slowly stood up and motioned for Saralia to move forward into the clearing. They quietly approached the wall, and Victoria quickly climbed onto Saralia's shoulders and could barely see over the top of the wall. When her eyes adjusted to the light, she nearly gasped in shock with what she saw.

There stood a Kittrian village like the others she had seen, but the trees that were normally standing around the village had been recently cut down, and their stumps were still burning. A few houses had been burned down as well, and the main gates were lying on the ground as if something big had smashed them open. The bodies of a few Kittrian guards lay on the ground on the pathways and in doorways. Then, she noticed a large group of Kittrians and a few Blakmian prisoners a few hundred feet from the gate were being marched away in chains. They were surrounded by hundreds of gritters and a few greatures.

"What do you see?" Saralia whispered.

"They're taking the last of the prisoners away to the south."

"Well, we should rescue them, then!"

"There are literally hundreds of gritters and nearly two dozen greatures. We don't stand much of a chance."

"Well, that is no good. What do we do now?"

Victoria looked back over the wall, and this time, a particular greature caught her eye. Not only was he wearing full plate armor, but he had an old ragged red cape and a battered-but-somewhat-fancy helmet.

"I think I can see the leader," Victoria said. "If we want to get any information, I bet we could get it out of him."

"So how do we catch him?"

"I'm going to climb over the wall and try to ambush him. You should make your way to another gate and try and get in from that way. There's too many at the main gate."

"Alright. Good luck."

Victoria stabbed her claws into the wood wall and quickly climbed over it. She paused on the top of the wall for only a second before leaping down onto the wooden roof of a house. She worked her way across the rooftops until she got close enough to the greature to hear what he was saying.

"I want you to take the prisoners to the tunnel. I have a special case I need to see to before I leave," the armored greature hissed to some gritters that were following him.

The gritters turned and started to run away but were struck down by two arrows that came from down the street. The greature looked at the fallen gritters in surprise, but before he could do anything, Victoria had jumped off of the roof and landed on his shoulders, knocking him off balance, and he fell to the ground. Victoria held her claws to the beast's throat as Saralia galloped down the road, her scimitars drawn, to deal with some gritters who had come out of a house to try and aid their leader. The greature tried to move away, but Victoria stabbed its right leg with the claws on her left hand and kept the claws on her right at the beast's neck.

"Where are you taking those prisoners?" Victoria growled through clenched teeth.

But before the greature could answer, a small knife flew through the air and embedded itself into the greature's forehead, killing him instantly. Victoria looked up and caught a glimpse of a figure dressed in dark blue vanishing over the wall.

She pulled her claws out of the dead greature as Saralia galloped over.

"The prisoners are all gone!" she said, panting for breath.

"I heard him mention a tunnel. Maybe in the mountain range to the south?"

"Maybe. I didn't see any passageway, though. Maybe they...."

Just then, Saralia was cut off by Victoria, who held up her hand.

"Did you hear that?"

"Hear what?"

The two listened for a moment before they heard it again.

"Help me!"

The cry for help was followed by a girlish scream.

"There's someone over there!" Victoria shouted, and the two rushed over to a house.

"Hold on! We are coming!" Saralia shouted.

Victoria tried the door handle as the two heard another scream from inside the house but found it was locked.

"Let me try," Saralia said as she backed up to the door and brought it down with one solid kick from her hind legs.

Victoria rushed into the house and saw a gritter standing by a cot, its clawed hands reaching out towards a Kittrian girl trying to cover herself with a dirty sheet.

"Get away from her!" Victoria screamed as she lunged at the gritter.

Before he could even turn around, Victoria had impaled him through the back with both of her claws, lifting him into the air and then flinging him across the room into a wall, where he crumpled into a heap. Saralia stepped into the room, ducking under the low ceiling.

"Tori? Is that you?" the child whispered before passing out.

Victoria gasped and pulled her claws off before gently removing the sheet to reveal the dirty face of a young girl with long white hair.

"The One Above! She is only a child!" Saralia said as she made her way over and began to pull out her pouch of healing herbs and bandages.

"Not just any child; it's Annalio, Groman's sister!" Victoria said in shock.

EARLIER, THE THREE men waved at Saralia and Victoria as they trotted away.

"Could we hurry?" Groman asked. "I do not want to waste any time."

"Hold on tight, then!" Trakken shouted as he took off at full gallop.

By noon, they caught sight of light reflecting off of a body of water.

"That is the Ice River! It is a few miles ahead, but we should make it there before I am completely worn out!" Trakken panted as they rushed along.

Soon, they stopped by the river. Trakken came to a stop, and his riders jumped off. Trakken breathlessly walked over to a tree that stood near the river and laid down in its shade. Groman walked over to the riverbank and sat down in the sand. Stephen walked over to him and sat down next to him.

"You know, there is a chance we may have to fight," Stephen said in a low voice as he tossed a stone into the river.

"I know you and Trakken can handle yourselves," Groman replied calmly.

"Groman, do you mind if I ask you why you don't want to fight?"

Groman sighed and looked at Stephen.

"When I was younger, and my sister was only a few years old, my family was traveling to Areiop for a big festival, when we were attacked by a swarm of gritters. My parents did their best to protect Annie and myself, but they were quickly overwhelmed. Then, some archers who were traveling from Areiop heard the fight, and they hurried over to help. They were young, reckless, inexperienced, and looking for something to try their new, illegal poisoned arrows on, when they heard us screaming for help. Sadly, they were not very good with their weapons, and while they did finish off the other gritters, my parents were caught in the crossfire. They died there, on the trail, in my arms, while my sister watched."

"Thankfully, she does not remember much of the incident. It was because of people being eager to kill that my parents needlessly died. From then on, I told myself that I wouldn't become a killer like those archers. Even when the leaders from Areiop brought the Empty Sword to my village, discovered that I was able to wield it, and took me away from my sister and my village so I could train in Areiop, I have continued to hold to that commitment."

Stephen looked at his companion in shock.

"Groman, I'm so sorry that this horrible thing happened to you. I agree that war does often hurt many people who get caught in the crossfire, but I can also say that if it weren't for those archers, you may not be alive today."

"So you are saying I should be grateful to those foolish men who murdered my parents?"

"Not exactly. Whatever shape war is in, there will be casualties, and while it is normally up to the leaders, it is the soldier who can be the biggest difference in how many people die. I don't like killing, myself, but I will fight to protect my family and my friends. If I don't, who will? Ask yourself: what would happen if the soldiers stopped fighting?"

"We would be overrun and enslaved by The Shadowed One's forces."

"Right."

"*They* would still be alive, though. Better to be a living slave than to die on the battlefield."

"They would be slaves under the rule of a tyrant who doesn't care if they are dead or alive. He might just kill them for the mere fun of it! Where I come from, we have had many evil rulers rise up to try and conquer the world in our history. Do you know what happened? Those that surrendered without a fight were normally oppressed to near extinction, while others fought seemingly impossible odds and yet they did win in the end. And in this world, it is no different. We face a foe that wants to crush everyone beneath his feet. If he wanted to spare Falamore, don't you think he'd still be around today? That just means that The Shadowed One is out to kill and destroy, and it's up to us to stop him."

"I do not know...."

"Think about it. But don't take too long; war doesn't tend to wait around for people to make up their minds."

Stephen got up and walked over to Trakken, who was still breathing hard.

"How are you holding up?" he asked.

"Just give me a few more minutes, and we can keep going," Trakken responded.

After Trakken was rested enough to continue, the trio crossed the river and pressed onward towards their goal. As the sun was beginning to set, the three warriors spotted the stone walls of Gadwar, surrounded by the southern range.

"There it is!" Trakken panted as they approached.

"Good! Wait here, Groman, and I will approach on foot!" Stephen shouted as they came to a halt.

Groman and Stephen slid off Trakken, who slowly walked over to a tree and laid down in the shade. As the two men slowly walked up to the city, Stephen looked over the terrain: it was mostly made of steep hills, with rocks jutting out at odd angles in different places. Gadwar itself was built into the side of the mountain range, with the walls ending where the mountains began.

However, he couldn't shake the feeling that something was off.

"Should there be guards or at least a few gritters standing around?" Groman asked.

"My thoughts exactly. Let's see if we can get inside and figure out what's going on," Stephen replied as the two hurried over to the main gate, only to find it had been bashed down by a formidable force and lying on the outside of the wall.

Groman slowly walked over to the fallen gate and looked it over. "What do you think could have done this?" he asked. "The hills are a little steep for a battering ram."

"No. A ram would have been on the outside and knocked the gate inward. I know what did this," Stephen replied as he walked over to the other gate and pointed out a large dent in the wood. "That is the size of an Unkarian fist. I should know; I got an up-close look at one in Altimi."

"You mean this was knocked down by a person?"

"Not just any person; the Unkarians are huge and very strong."

The two men walked over the fallen gates and went inside the city. It was a modestly-sized town with stone houses and thatched roofs. A marketplace was in the center, and there was what looked to be a mineshaft dug into the mountainside.

"This place is abandoned. Everybody is gone," Groman said with a worried look.

"We don't know that yet. Let's look around and check the houses; there may be someone or something left behind," Stephen replied.

Soon, the two were running house to house, looking through open doors or windows, trying to see if they could find any survivors. Sadly, they only found a few dead gritters and the bodies of Kittrian, Trodontian, and Blakmian guards. Groman insisted they take care of the fallen, so they built a pyre and cremated the dead soldiers.

As they watched the fire burn, Trakken joined them in the town, and they searched the city again in the moonlight. Finding nothing, they picked a house and slept inside.

The next morning, Stephen was up before the others and was looking around again, when the mineshaft caught his eye.

He walked over to the entrance and peered inside. He could see that there was indeed a shaft going down into the mountain, and it was lit by still-burning torches along the walls. He drew his sword, pulled his shield off of his back, and slowly crept into the dim tunnel.

After walking for a while, he heard some voices coming from deeper into the mine and hurried over to where the sound came from as quietly as he could. He soon spotted a junction in the tunnel going in different directions: a tunnel going to the left and right and a different shaft going deeper still into the dark abyss.

A greature dressed in full armor and wearing a ratty red cape was talking to a group of gritters at the tunnel intersection. Stephen ducked behind a large boulder and listened to the conversation.

"Our master wants the rest of his slaves brought to him, now. Go into the lower caves, take them to the staging point at Altimi, and wait there for further instructions. I have to take the tunnel to Jeatut and deal with a problematic slave."

The gritters hurried into the shaft, disappearing into the darkness. Stephen was about to attack the lone greature when he spotted something coming up from the shaft: it was the same cat-like creature he had seen at Altimi.

"What do you want, hairball?" the greature hissed.

"I am coming with you to make sure you do not make another mistake," Ripper purred menacingly.

"Fine; just do not get in my way."

The two enemies walked down the tunnel and disappeared.

Stephen checked to make sure no one else was watching and quietly made his way back to the surface.

Soon, he could see sunlight coming in through the entrance, and he spotted Groman waiting for him.

"Find anything down there?" Groman asked.

"Yeah. They're taking the slaves to Altimi through a tunnel. Apparently, they have tunnels from Altimi to Jeatut!"

"So that is how they managed to attack so quickly and catch everybody by surprise."

"Sounds like it. Where's Trakken?"

"Still sleeping. I think he may be asleep for a few more hours after the hard journey yesterday. We should let him get as much rest as possible before moving on."

"Alright, but let's make sure the gritters can't come back through this tunnel."

The two of them built a barricade out of anything they could find and blocked the entrance of the mine.

By the time they had finished completely blocking the hole in the ground, it was late afternoon, and they were exhausted. They both went back into the house they had spent the night in and were soon asleep once more.

The three woke up just as the sun was beginning to rise. Stephen and Groman told Trakken what they knew, and the three of them decided to make their way back to Prariat.

They went at a slower pace but were still able to make it back to the city a few hours after dark. There, they found Windmere waiting for them at the gates.

"Where have you been?!" she shouted.

"Did Galent or Elder Gilder explain?" Groman asked as he slipped off of Trakken's back.

"Yes, they did. What city did you go to?"

"Gadwar," Trakken responded.

"Did you find anything?"

"We know what happened to the townsfolk but nothing more," Stephen replied. "Are Tori and Saralia back yet?"

"Not yet. Let us go talk to Galent and Elder Gilder and explain to them what you know."

The four of them went over to the great hall, where they recounted their story in full.

After they had answered every question the two leaders had, they were allowed to go to Windmere's home to rest.

Stephen's sleep was fitful. He was worried about his sister, and he prayed that she would be alright.

THE NEXT MORNING, STEPHEN was awakened by a shout outside the house.

"I need help!"

Stephen jumped out of his bed and hurried outside.

He saw Saralia slowly stumbling into the smithy, nearly faint from exhaustion. Victoria was still on her back; she was tightly holding something wrapped in cloth in her arms. Before Saralia completely gave out, Victoria slid off her back and hurried inside the house just as Windmere came rushing out, and she and Stephen helped Saralia inside.

Trakken quickly cleared the table, and Victoria gently laid the bundle on it. He couldn't help but gasp when he saw what she was carrying: it was Annie, wearing a dirty brown dress that was stained and torn; her face was bruised, and a bit of dried blood was under her nose.

"Groman, get in here!" Victoria shouted.

Groman came out of the bedroom and looked at the scene in shock.

"Annie! What have those monsters done to you?!" he shouted as he rushed over. Annie barely turned her head towards her brother's voice and managed a weak smile when she saw him before letting her sadness show when she noticed his horrified face.

"I tried to escape; they did not like that. They made sure I would not run away again," Annie said weakly before passing out.

Victoria walked over to Groman and put her hands on his shoulders.

"Groman, I'm sorry. I need you to be strong for her sake," she said in a firm but quiet voice.

"What are you talking about? You got her back alive! That is all that matters to me!" he said rather loudly.

Victoria said nothing but walked over to Annie's still body and slowly lifted the hem of Annie's dress.

There was an audible gasp from everyone in the room as they saw that where Annie's lower legs and feet should have been, there were now only two bandaged stumps.

Chapter 12. Training.

The next few hours were a blur of activity. Windmere and Trakken were trying to take care of Saralia, who was too tired to even stand, having run at full speed the entire night, while Groman, Victoria, and Stephen tried their best to see to Annie's wounds.

When they were finished cleaning and dressing Annie's injuries, they gently laid her in a cot that had been hastily erected by Trakken. After making sure Annie was asleep and not in any more pain, Groman went outside and sat down on an anvil. Victoria and Stephen followed him but kept at a distance.

"Will she be alright?" Victoria asked quietly, her eyes still wet with tears.

"She will live, thanks in no small part to your efforts. But...." Groman's voice trailed off as he placed his head in his hands and started to quietly cry.

"She won't be able to walk again, will she?" Stephen said quietly.

Groman stood up quickly and picked up his sword from the workbench, where he had left it the night before, and pulled it from its sheath. He pointed it downwards and plunged the blade deep into the earth with a scream of fury and frustration.

"I wish I had never left Fruniet! I could have saved her!" he shouted in a rage. "If I was not The Chosen One, none of this would have happened!"

Stephen walked over to Groman and placed his hand on his shoulder.

"A wise man in our world once said, 'there are no ifs in God's world.' I don't know much about The One Above I've heard you mention many times, but if he is anything like our God, then I know that he has a plan in all of this, as tough as it may seem. Sometimes God puts us through tough times to test and strengthen us. Don't blame yourself; you're not the one who cut her legs off below the knee. That is the Shadowed One's fault; if anything, it should make you want to go after him even more."

"But I do not want to kill anyone," Groman said quietly.

"Neither do I, but I am willing to do so if I have to defend myself or my friends. As noble of an idea as pacifism is, it can only prosper during peacetime. When you refuse to fight, you let anyone else come in and do whatever they want to you and your family. Sometimes, you need to rise up and defend what matters most. And, at times, that means killing the one who is threatening you."

Groman pulled away from Stephen, and walked over to his sword that was still sticking out of the ground and pulled it out, looking at the shiny blade.

"If that is what it will take to keep my sister safe...so be it. When do we start?"

"As soon as we can get an army ready," Windmere said as she stepped out from the house into the smithy. "Once I came to from the drugs Saralia had given me, I went over to Chief Galent and Elder Gilder, and we have been devising a plan of attack. We are currently building siege weapons and calling up as many soldiers as we can muster. We march on the Black Peak in a week. Until then, I would suggest that you two teach Groman how to fight. We need everyone to be ready for the coming battle."

THE NEXT FEW DAYS WERE also a blur. The Trodontians were busy building catapults and trebuchets, and every day, more soldiers joined the growing army. Stephen and Victoria took turns training Groman in sword fighting and hand-to-hand combat.

During their training sessions, Annie would be brought outside in a chair to watch her big brother and cheer him on. Despite her loss, she was always cheerful and did everything she could to encourage Groman and everyone around her. After a few days, Trakken completed a crude wheelchair for her, and she was soon wheeling herself around and trying to help wherever she could.

Groman was a fast learner, and the twins soon had him to an acceptable level of confidence with his blade and his fists.

Late one morning, after five days of preparation, the twins were working with Groman again when they heard a screech from overhead. They looked up and saw some Blakmians flying down towards them.

"Hello, there, young warriors!" one of the birdmen called out. "Are you The Chosen Ones we have heard tales about?"

"Why do you ask?" Stephen inquired as he raised his sword in a defensive stance. Victoria followed by drawing her claws out of their sheaths, and Groman stepped in front of Annie with his sword at the ready.

"We come to ask for your aid. We are merchants and traders who were bringing some weapons and supplies to aid your cause, when we were ambushed by some of our own kin who were in the service of The Shadowed One. They took our supplies and left them at their camp on the banks of the Ice River. We would retrieve them ourselves, but we are not skilled in combat like you. Could you lend us a hand? You can have all the supplies you want."

"Let us discuss the matter. In the meantime, could you stay right there while we talk?" Victoria said.

"Certainly. We mean no harm to any of you. We are willing to do whatever it takes to get our supplies back and help your cause," the leader of the group replied as the heroes turned to each other.

"I'm almost certain it's a trap," Stephen said coldly. "We should capture them now and let the leaders deal with them."

"What if it is not? They may really need our help," Groman responded.

"We need to figure out if they are on our side," Victoria said.

Just then, the group heard a familiar voice overhead.

"Good morning, all," Vulant said as he landed near the group. The Blakmian merchants, upon seeing Vulant, quickly bowed.

"King Vulant, it is good to see you again," the leader of the merchants said.

"Hello, Shriken. It has been a while, and please stop with this 'king' business. I may be heir to my father's throne, but I cannot be king until Altimi is back in our hands once more."

"Of course, sir," Shriken said as he and his merchants stood up. "We were asking The Chosen Ones for their assistance in retrieving some goods that were stolen from us by some traitorous Blakmian mercenaries."

"What kind of goods?"

"We were bringing weapons we scavenged from battlefields in Altimi. The city has been completely abandoned, save for the fallen heroes who tried to defend it, after the Shadowed One took over. After making sure the bodies of the fallen were properly buried—with all honor we could bestow, of course—we searched the palace and found something that our fallen king Falamore had left for you."

"Vulant, you know these men?" Stephen asked.

"Shriken is an old friend," Vulant replied. "If he says they have weapons for us, he will not be lying."

"Alright. We will help you," Groman said, putting his sword in its sheath and stepping forward with his hand outstretched. Shriken took his hand and shook it.

"Thank you," Shriken said with another bow.

"I hope we won't regret this," Victoria said to Stephen in a whisper.

"Me too."

Just after noon—after gathering some supplies and each of them getting a hug from Annie—the trio, joined by Vulant, the Blakmian merchants, Trakken, Saralia, and Windmere set out southwards to find the stolen goods.

The journey was uneventful, and, at dusk, they spotted the traitor's camp. The small army charged, and most of the Blakmians took off in fear upon seeing their opponents; the few that stayed were quickly subdued and tied to a tree.

The team quickly went about and looked over the stolen loot that they had recaptured. As they looked over the barrels of arrows and piles of swords, Shriken came over to Vulant with something wrapped in a leather bundle.

"This is what we found in the palace armory. It had a note for you left on it, and we have not read it, as we wanted to get it to you right away," Shriken said with a bow.

Vulant took the bundle, looked at the note, and read it out loud:

My dear son Vulant,

I am sorry for what my passing has put you through. I am certain that my revelation of my true nature was hard enough as it is. However, we cannot dwell on our past; we can only live in the present and look to the future. I can see that you will be a fine king of the Blakmian people, and I will be watching your glorious rule from the realm in the sky. I am not only leaving you the throne but this token, given to me by my father, to prove your rule to anyone who dares question it. Wield it well, my son. And may The One Above give you many years of peace and prosperity.

Your loving father,

Falamore

Vulant carefully placed the letter in a pocket of his breeches and gently unwrapped the bundle. Inside, he found a hand-and-a-half sword in its scabbard. Its golden hilt was beautifully crafted, with a sky-blue jewel set into the cross-guard. Vulant slowly pulled the sword from the scabbard, his eyes wide with amazement. The golden sword seemed to glow in the fading sunlight.

"This is the king's sword. It supposedly went missing after the prince, my father, vanished."

"Looks like he hid it until he found someone worthy to use it," Stephen said.

"I am not worthy of this," Vulant said as he put the sword back into its scabbard.

"All the more reason you are, my king," Shriken said.

Vulant sighed and strapped the sword onto his back.

"I am too tired to think about this now. Let us set up camp and head back to the army in the morning."

Saralia yawned. "Sounds like a plan to me."

After getting their tents set up, most of the group were soon asleep; however, Victoria lay awake, trying to figure out how to best Groman in their next training session.

As she was deep in thought, she heard a voice coming from outside her tent.

"Tori! Help me!"

She quickly sat up on her sleeping mat and looked around and, seeing nothing, decided she was just hearing things.

"Tori! Help!"

"Annie?!" she called out into the darkness.

"Tori!" the voice came again.

Victoria quickly grabbed her Tekko-Kagi claws and raced out of her tent.

"Wake up, everybody! Annie needs help!" she shouted at her sleeping companions as she sprinted past them.

"Help me, Tori!" the voice was coming from a patch of woods nearby.

Victoria didn't waste a second and ran into the darkness. She eventually came to where the river ran through the trees and stopped to catch her breath.

"Annie! Where are you?! How did you leave Prariat?!" she shouted into the blackness.

Suddenly, she heard something whistling towards her head, and she instinctively ducked. A small dart hit the sand a short distance away from her, missing her head by inches. She pulled her Tekko-Kagi claws out and scanned the trees, but the shadows were too thick.

"Your devotion towards your friend is admirable," a smooth voice purred from the shadows.

"If you've hurt her in any way, I swear I will gut you like a fish," Victoria growled as she turned around, trying to locate where the voice was coming from.

"Do not worry. I do not have her, because I am not looking for her. I have come for you."

"When my friends get here, you won't stand a chance."

"That may be true if I have not put them all to sleep with my sleeping darts. Alas, you dodged my last one, so I will have to take you the hard way."

Victoria turned just in time to see a rock come flying out of a tree. She dodged the missile, only to see a figure clad in blue jump out of a different tree and pounce at her. It had gauntlets made of a black metal that were tipped with extremely sharp claws. Victoria held up her own claws, and the weapons clashed with a resounding clang.

"Your reflexes are impressive," the figure said as he leaped backward and away from her.

"Come closer, and you can find out just how good they are, Bomski!" Victoria shouted.

The assassin frowned. "I prefer Ripper," the cat-like ninja said with a low growl before attacking again.

The two fighters began a heated duel, Tekko-Kagi against metal-tipped claws: his attack; her counter; her kick; his dodge. They kept exchanging blows in the dim moonlight, with Victoria taking a few kicks from Ripper, but she refused to back down. After taking a backhand to the face, Victoria nearly lost her balance but was up again in seconds and launched another attack.

"I grow tired of this," Ripper said as he dodged Victoria's wide swipe and countered with his own, causing her to fall back.

"Feel free to surrender anytime," Victoria responded as she raised her weapons again.

Ripper pounced with his claws outstretched. Victoria blocked the attack with her weapons but saw Ripper's tail come at her face like a scorpion's. She felt a sharp pain in her neck and backed away. She could feel a few drops of warm blood running down her neck, from where the sharp tip on Ripper's tail had cut her neck like a paper cut, and onto her tunic.

"You won't do that again," she said as she attacked.

But as she charged, Ripper simply stepped aside, and she stumbled past him.

"I will not need to. The sleeping powder I coated my tail tip with is taking effect already. Soon, you will be too tired to stand," Ripper said with a smile.

"We'll see about that!" Victoria shouted as she charged again.

This time, as Ripper stepped away, she swung her left claw in his direction and managed to tear a hole in his trousers. Before she managed to attack again, she stumbled and fell onto the sandy riverbank.

As her vision faded, she watched Ripper stand over her and smile.

"You fought well, young one. Do not worry. I do not plan to kill you. The Shadowed One wants you alive."

Victoria was soon asleep on the riverbank, and her Amronian captor tied her up and began to carry her off into the night.

Chapter 13. Betrayal.

Victoria was awakened by some cold water being splashed on her face. She saw Ripper standing by her and immediately began to kick and scream, only to find her hands and feet had been bound, and she had a cloth gag in her mouth.

"Good morning. Or should I say good afternoon? You slept for quite some time last night and into this morning," Ripper said with a calm smile as Victoria glared daggers back at him. "Do not worry. I will take the gag off in a little while. I just needed to rest for a moment."

Ripper then picked up Victoria with surprising strength and tossed her over his shoulder.

He began to run at a quick pace through the woods along the Ice River. Soon, they came to a clearing, where Ripper stopped and gently set Victoria on the ground.

"We are very far away from your friends. Nobody can hear you. But I would prefer you do not scream; it may make your situation worse. Do I have your word you will not scream?"

Victoria sighed through the gag and nodded. With one swipe of his claws, Ripper cut the gag off. Victoria took a few deep breaths of fresh air and looked at her kidnapper.

"Why are you taking me instead of Groman?" she asked.

"It is all a part of his master plan. Even I do not know what he intends to do with you. I merely do what I am told."

"Did you kidnap Annie? I heard her voice last night."

"Oh, did you, Tori?" Ripper asked, his voice a perfect impersonation of Annie's.

Victoria looked at him in shock.

"Voice mimicry is a specialty of most Amronians such as myself. Do you have any more questions?"

"Just one: did you cut off Annie's legs? I know you were at Jeatut; I saw you kill the greature I was trying to get some info out of."

Ripper looked at her in surprise and genuine shock.

"Is that what the greature did? I knew Red Cape was going to punish the little girl, but I did not think that he would do something like that." He looked away from Victoria, almost as if he was ashamed. "I am so sorry. Is she...?"

"Alive? Yes, though no thanks to you. She will never walk again."

Ripper went silent and took a few steps away.

"Enough of that. I am going to take you to the top of that hill over there," Ripper said pointing to a small, wooded rise. "There, I will tie you to a tree until nightfall, when we can travel again. If you think about trying to call for help, do not bother; your friends are long gone by now."

As the sun was beginning to set in the west, Ripper carried Victoria over a large tree on the top of a hill and bound her to its thick trunk.

Just as he was finishing tightening the ropes in front of her, she saw a small figure dressed in a dark green hooded cloak and trousers appear in a tree behind them. She crouched down like a cat, with her black tail rapidly swishing back and forth. After a few seconds, she let out a scream that reminded Victoria of a cougar, as she pounced at Ripper's back.

Ripper spun around at lightning speed, only to be knocked off his padded feet by a small Amronian child. The two of them rolled on the grass before coming to a stop, with Ripper grabbing the child's shoulders.

"I got you, Daddy!" the child purred playfully as Ripper helped her up and hugged her. The child was very similar to Ripper except she was covered in black fur, all except for her left hand, which was white as snow, and she had bright orange eyes that sparkled with excitement.

"You most certainly did, little one. But why are you here? I told you: Daddy has work to do," Ripper said while playfully messing with his child's hood.

"Mommy says she has dinner ready for you and that you better not say no to her a third time."

"Alright. I will be there shortly, my little Hannela. Now, run along and help your mommy."

"Okay, Daddy!" the little girl said as she disappeared into the forest, her green cloak and black tail streaming out behind her.

Ripper turned back to Victoria.

"I am sorry for the intrusion. My daughter likes to try and ambush me whenever I am near my home."

"She seems to take after you."

"Actually, she gets her excellent hunting skills and her black fur from her mother. I merely help her hone her natural talents."

Ripper stepped away from Victoria and began to walk back down the hill in the direction his daughter had disappeared.

"I am going to leave you here for a little while. I will be back in a few hours; I trust you will not go anywhere."

"I wouldn't even know where to go if I could."

"Good girl. I will see you in a while. If you do not cause trouble, I might just bring you some food."

With that, Ripper took off down the hill and disappeared.

Victoria quickly tried to wiggle free of the ropes but to no avail.

"Looks like I will have to wait after all," she said to herself.

As she waited, she wondered how long it would take for her friends and her brother to figure out where she was, much less come to her rescue. She thought about all her adventures in that world thus far, the people she had met, and the battles she had fought. She thought about how to defeat Groman the next time they sparred if they would ever fight again. She wondered what The Shadowed One had planned for her. Did he plan to use her as bait? Leverage? Or maybe he just wanted to kill her himself? She shuddered at the thought of his huge sword coming down on her head.

Suddenly, a voice snapped her out of her thoughts.

"Since you have been a good girl, I brought some leftovers," Ripper purred from behind her, making her jump in surprise. He then walked around the tree and faced her before pulling some roasted meat from a cloth pouch. "You have two choices: I untie one of your arms, but only if you do not try to fight or run away, or I can feed them to you and leave you in your bonds for a while longer. Which do you prefer?"

"I won't fight back. It would only make my situation worse."

"Smart girl."

Ripper gently untied her right arm and handed her the food which she gladly took. After eating, Ripper tied her arms again and untied her feet.

"I am going to let you walk with me this time. Carrying you earlier was not as easy as I thought."

Victoria ignored the insult and waited for her legs to be freed. She knew she might be able to get one kick in before he realized his mistake; she had to make it count.

But before she could enable her plan, the sound of a horn split the evening air. Ripper looked up with surprise, his cat-like ears turning towards the sound.

"Those are the warning horns! My village is under attack!" he shouted as he jumped up.

"Wait! Let me help you!" Victoria shouted.

"And let you escape? No. However, I cannot take the chance of someone finding you here, so you will have to come with me."

With one swipe of his metal claws, Ripper cut the ropes that bound her to the tree but left the ropes around her hands and fastened a guiding line to them. Ripper then took off at a full sprint, with Victoria struggling to keep up, the guide rope pulling her along.

They came to the top of a hill, and there, Victoria saw the village. There were no walls, and most of the houses were built like log cabins, while the others were stone. But many of them were on fire, the flames lighting up the sky. She could see many Amronians running around, some trying to stop the fires and others fighting their attackers. She looked in surprise when she saw the silhouettes of one of the invaders in the streets: it was a greature calling in dozens of gritters as they swarmed the town's defenders.

"No! He cannot do this!" Ripper screamed over the chaos below them. He began to run away down the hill, but Victoria pulled back on the guide rope, making him stop.

"Please, let me help you. You can't do it alone."

Ripper didn't hesitate; he cut her bonds and pulled out Victoria's Tekko-Kagi claws from a leather bag on his belt, tossing them to her.

"My family will be in the stone house on the north side. Please try and protect them. I am going to find whoever started this and kill them," Ripper growled before letting out a lion-like roar and racing down the hill on all fours, with Victoria close behind him.

Ripper quickly approached a cluster of gritters who had a female Amronian cornered by a house. Just before he came to them, he let out a scream like a cougar, and by the time the gritters turned towards him, it was already too late. They were swiftly killed, and Ripper turned to his next victims, slashing his way through the swarm with the claws on his hands and feet and the blade on his tail.

Victoria entered the town and ran northwards, looking for the stone house Ripper had described to her. She soon spotted a modest stone building at the end of the street, with three greatures standing at the door trying to smash their way in. She quickly fought her way through a small group of gritters before approaching the greatures. She got a running start and jumped towards them with her arms outstretched. She killed the two greatures on the left and right with her claws and her body slammed into the middle one, causing him to fall into the door, which finally gave way. She pulled out her claws from the dead greatures and quickly killed the remaining one in the middle before he had time to get up.

She then looked into the house and saw three Amronian children, including Hannela, huddled in the corner with whom she assumed to be their mother standing in front of them, ready to defend her children.

The mother growled jond started to charge at Victoria, who quickly lowered her weapons and stepped back.

"Wait! I'm here to help you! Bomski sent me to get you out of here while he deals with the leader of this attack."

The mother stopped and looked at Victoria. Her fierce blue eyes went from a look of rage to one of surprise as she backed down.

"If my husband sent you, then he knows you will do your best to help, and if he says it will be best if we leave, then so be it," she said before going over to the children, who were still huddled in the corner of the room. She whispered something to them. They quickly got behind her, and Victoria led them out of the house and into the chaos outside.

Many houses were burning at this point, and while dozens of gritters and greatures lay dead in the street, still more kept coming in from the south. Victoria and the mother fought side-by-side, clawing their way through the horde, trying to get out of the town.

Just as they saw the edge of the village, the wall of a house they were passing burst open, and debris flew everywhere. A plank hit Victoria square in the chest and knocked her to the ground. She looked up and saw a huge figure step through what was left of the flaming house and approach the mother and children, who were all on the ground in a daze.

"Get away from them!" Victoria screamed as she jumped to her feet and lunged at the giant, who turned and knocked her aside with a heavy gauntlet. She slammed into a house and fell to the ground, gasping for air.

The giant laughed in a deep, booming voice.

"Look what I found here: one of The Chosen Ones. Back for another beating? I thought you had learned your lesson after my lord had defeated you and the fool who was calling himself a king. Now, I, Thaliton, will finally get to have some fun with all of you."

He stooped low and reached for the smallest of the Amronian children, when a scream like a wildcat's caught his attention, and he looked up just in time to see Ripper, his green eyes blazing with rage, leaping from a burning rooftop.

Ripper caught the giant's neck with his left hand and swung around it, digging his claws into the monster's throat as his inertia carried him around the neck and onto the giant's shoulders. Blood poured from Thaliton's throat, and he sagged to his knees, trying to stop the blood flow with his hands. Ripper quickly turned his attention to the back of Thaliton's neck and began slashing wildly at the exposed skin, cutting deeper and deeper. Thaliton let out a gurgled moan and fell on his face. Ripper quickly grabbed his fallen opponent's dagger and stabbed him in the back of his head, causing the huge Unkarian to go limp.

"That is what you get for betraying me and trying to hurt my family!" he screamed as he stood on top of the fallen Unkarian general.

A few seconds later, the sounds of glass breaking and chains clinking got the warrior's attention as a large chained shield smashed through a window and towards Ripper. He jumped up and managed to land on the shield as it was being pulled back and leap towards The Shadowed One as he crashed through another house. Ripper roared again as he flew towards his giant opponent, his claws on his hands and feet poised and the blade on his tail ready to strike. He landed on The Shadowed One's chest and sank his claws into any soft spot he could find while trying to slash at the giant's neck with his tail.

The Shadowed One laughed as Ripper hung by his claws on his chest. With one motion, The Shadowed One dropped the Ruler's Sword and grabbed Ripper with a huge hand and squeezed. Ripper let out a howl of pain and was thrown at his family, who were just getting to their feet, knocking them all to the ground again.

"You cannot win, assassin, and you know it!" The Shadowed One taunted as he loomed over Ripper, who was struggling to his feet.

Victoria stood up and looked over at the Amronian family; she noticed one was missing. She quickly glanced around and spotted Hannela silently creeping around to get behind The Shadowed One.

Victoria also crept behind the monster as he was busy taunting Ripper and motioned for Hannela to follow her lead. Together, they positioned themselves behind the giant's legs, and they slashed the back of his knees with their claws at the same time. The Shadowed One let out a roar of surprise and pain as his legs buckled, and he fell, catching himself with his hands. Before anyone could take advantage of the fallen giant's vulnerability, he swung himself up on his hands and kicked back with his legs, knocking Hannela and Victoria into a wall, where they both crumpled into a heap. Ripper was on his feet now but was swiftly swatted aside by the monster's huge hand. There was a sickening crunch when Ripper's body smashed into a tree, where he fell and slumped over.

Victoria looked up to see the fallen body of Ripper lying at an unnatural angle against a house and the tip of the Ruler's Sword in her face.

"At least Ripper did not fail in bringing you to me. Now, I can finish what I set out to do!" The Shadowed One laughed as dozens of gritters swarmed around her and her friends, the ground rumbling with the noise of all of them running around. The Shadowed One raised his sword and prepared to drive its blade into her chest. Victoria closed her eyes and braced herself for the end.

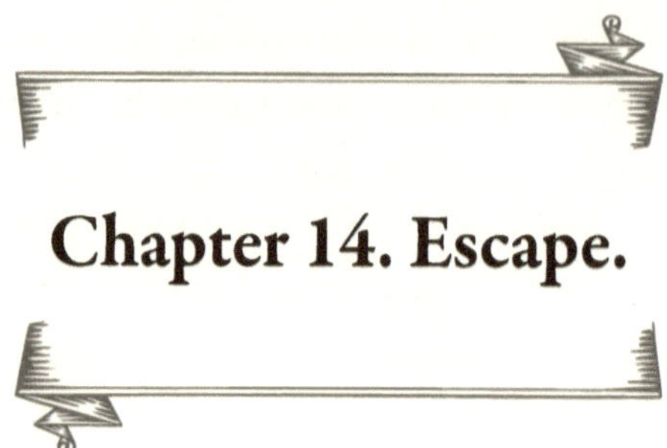

Chapter 14. Escape.

Victoria waited for her demise, her eyes shut in fear as the huge blade began to plunge at her.

Suddenly, she heard the sound of a large object whistling through the air and a loud *thunk*!

She opened her eyes and saw The Shadowed One falling to the ground, his face having been crushed by a bloody war hammer that was lying on the ground in front of him. She then realized that the rumbling she heard was the thunder of hooves and running feet, as the Trodontian cavalry rushed onto the scene, sending the swarms of gritters running away in fear. She spotted Trakken racing over, his large two-handed broadsword drawn and ready to strike. Stephen was on his back, looking like a fully-armored knight with his sword and shield. She jumped up and ran over to her allies and was quickly scooped up by Windmere, while Saralia stood by with an arrow on her bowstring. Groman rode up on Chieftain Galent; both of them had their large swords drawn and ready for battle. She spotted Vulant and his Blakmian army hovering nearby, their archers poised and ready to fire a volley of arrows at their target. Some Kittrian soldiers materialized and quickly carried Ripper and his family away, while more appeared in the streets, cutting off any way of escape.

The Shadowed One stood up, his face already healing from its injury, and picked up the Ruler's sword and his chained shield. The second he did so, every soldier surrounding him drew their weapons and quickly surrounded him.

"Surrender," Chieftain Galent growled.

The Shadowed One smiled grimly as he looked at his enemies. "I surrender to no one."

"You are completely surrounded! Give up!" Groman shouted at him, the Empty Sword gleaming in the light from the burning houses and the triple moons.

"I may be, but so are you," the dark king laughed before blowing on a small stone horn. Immediately, the ground began to shake, and armored greatures began to burst from newly-created holes in the ground, while arrows began to rain from the sky, as the Shadowed One's own Blakmian mercenaries revealed themselves in the night sky and began to fire volley after volley into the crowds below. Vulant quickly turned his warriors against their traitorous brethren, and the sky became a massive air battle, while on the ground, all was chaos, as the soldiers were trying to fight off the emerging greatures and keep the Shadowed One from leaving.

The Shadowed One lowered his shield and charged straight at two Trodontian soldiers who were the closest to him, throwing them aside like toys as he barreled towards Groman and Chieftain Galent. The dark king swung the Ruler's Sword at Groman, who managed to deflect the blow with the Empty Sword with a resounding *clang*.

As more and more greatures kept coming from the holes in the ground, a call came out from Vulant.

"Retreat to the north! I and my warriors will try to cover you!"

"You heard the king! Retreat to the north!" Chieftain Galent's voice boomed as he and Groman took off at a gallop, trying to outpace The Shadowed One, who was still trying to get in close and finish them off. A few Trodontians tried to grab him and slow him down but were easily thrown aside for their pains.

However, in the seconds it took for The Shadowed One to defeat the brave warriors, the whole army was already moving away at top speed. As they galloped away, Windmere brought Victoria over to Trakken and Stephen.

"How did you get here so fast?!" Victoria shouted to her brother as the army raced through the dark forest.

"Easy. When we woke up, we found Ripper's calling card at our camp, and we knew we needed more help to rescue you. So we went back to Prariat and gathered the army, and we came here as fast as we could manage. When we got close, Trakken saw the Shadowed One about to run you through, he threw his hammer, and it hit him in his face. That brings us up to the present."

"I knew you'd come and find me."

"I have to ask: that dead Unkarian I saw back there; you were not the one to kill him, were you?" Saralia asked as she came up alongside the group.

"No, that was all Ripper's doing," Victoria said as her friends looked on in astonishment.

"No wonder The Shadowed One wanted him on his side," Trakken said.

"So what do we do now?!" Victoria shouted.

"Our plan is to encamp by the Ice Lake by the Northern Ice Range and prepare for a full assault on the Black Peak from there!" Stephen shouted back.

"Only one problem: we have to go past the ruined city of Cearit on the way. It is most undoubtedly a nest of wheelats by now," Windmere replied.

Saralia shivered, and Trakken turned pale. Stephen and Victoria looked at her in confusion.

"What are wheelats?" Stephen asked.

"Remember that huge creature you saw the Shadowed One riding in Altimi?" Trakken asked.

Stephen froze in fear and went as white as a sheet.

"I see why you're concerned," Victoria said. "Maybe if we can keep our pace up, we can get past them without any trouble."

"I hope so," Windmere said worriedly.

After they had been running for over an hour, the army began to slow down, and then finally stopped to regroup. As they gathered around and tried to catch their breath, a shadow fell across them, blocking the moonlight.

"Keep moving! Something is coming through the forest!" Vulant's voice shouted overhead. The Kittrian soldiers quickly vanished, and the Trodontians began to gallop northwards again.

As they raced along, Stephen noticed shadowy shapes running alongside them in the trees. To his horror, he saw that they were not only matching their own pace, but they were gaining on them.

Suddenly, a white blob came flying out at him. He held out his shield and felt a sticky substance hit it. He turned the shield over to see what looked like a slimy spider's web covering it. Before he could react, another blob flew out of the woods and caught him in the chest, knocking him off Trakken and onto the ground, dropping his sword in the process. He tried to get up but found his arms and legs were firmly stuck together by a mass of white silk. He tried to shout, but his mouth was covered in silk as well. He did his best to roll out of the way of oncoming Trodontians but was struck by one as he passed by, sending him bouncing over towards the trees.

He sighed in relief as he thought he was out of danger but then he heard a soft clicking sound and looked up to see what it was. To his sheer horror, a huge spider was crawling over to him, its red eyes glowing in the darkness. Stephen tried to get away but could only watch as the spider ran over to him and begin to wrap him up in even more silk.

When the spider bent down to pick him up, he became so scared, he blacked out in terror.

VICTORIA AND THE REST of the allied army continued their mad dash northwards through the night, trying to avoid hungry wheelats and smashing through the occasional gritter encampment. As the light of dawn began to light the sky above the mountains to the east, they came to a large lake nestled at the base of cold blue peaks. Victoria began to shiver as the air grew ever colder, and the army approached the lake and began to assemble along the shore.

"Set up camp! We will be safe here!" Chieftain Galent shouted to the army, who soon began to set up tents and lean-tos.

Victoria wandered over to Windmere, who was busy pounding tent pegs into the ground with a large wooden mallet.

"Are you sure we will be safe here?"

Windmere set down her mallet and looked over at her.

"Yes. The Shadowed One would not bother with us up here with the Ice Dwarves nearby. He should not be able to take on all of us in a pitched battle. And the ground is too frozen for his forces to tunnel underneath us."

"Ice Dwarves? Are they friendly?"

"Normally, they are, but sometimes, if you catch them at a bad moment, their being cold towards you is the least of your concerns."

"Do they live near here?"

"They live among the Northern Ice Range, across the lake from here. Sometimes, they used to travel down the Ice River to trade, but ever since the Fire Giants became more hostile towards them, they have since stopped."

"Do you think they will join in to help our army against the Shadowed One?"

"I do not know; they almost certainly know we are here and will undoubtedly come for a visit to see why we have come, but they normally are too busy dealing with the Fire Giants across the dividing range to help in a large conflict."

Victoria sighed and pulled her borrowed cloak tighter to herself, and she started to walk away when Trakken galloped over in a panic.

"Have either of you seen Stephen? He fell off me on the way up here. I hoped someone else had picked him up, but I cannot find him anywhere!" he panted.

"I have not seen him since our ambush at Felinad was overtaken," Windmere replied.

"He's probably making his way over here as we speak. He tends to fall behind whenever my family travels somewhere," Victoria said.

"That is what I hope for, but I also found this stuck to my saddlebag," Trakken said as he produced a small glob of a white substance.

Windmere trotted over and picked it up, then stretched it out in a long, white strand of goo.

"Wheelat silk...Stephen may be in bigger trouble than we thought," she said as she shook the glob from her hands.

"Are you saying he may have been caught by a wheelat?!" Victoria shouted.

"More than likely. Those bugs can spit silk at their prey with excellent accuracy. The silk binds them up, so they cannot fight back. Then, they take their helpless prey back to either their masters or their den," Trakken replied.

"Well, you mentioned a ruined city that was crawling with those things. Let's get the army together and go get him!" Victoria shouted as she grabbed her Tekko-Kagi claws and began to walk away.

"Easier said than done," Windmere said as she moved forward to block Victoria's path. "The army is too tired after our retreat last night, and the old city is going to be full of enemies. We need the army to be well-rested and ready before we go. I am sorry, Victoria, but we will have to wait."

"No! We need to get him, now!" Victoria exclaimed, ducking under Windmere's horse half and marching away. She only walked a few feet when a black-furred figure dressed in green and with a leather bag on its back raced out from behind a tent and into her, knocking them both onto the ground. When Victoria noticed its left hand was covered in white fur in contrast to the rest of its coal black fur, she realized it was eldest of Ripper's children.

"I am sorry! I did not know you were there!" the Amronian child cried as she leaped to her feet and helped Victoria up.

"That's alright. You're Hannela, right?" Victoria asked.

"Correct," Hannela purred happily. "I am glad you remembered. Daddy told me to give you this." She pulled the bag off of her back and held it out to Victoria, who took it, and before she opened it, she looked back at the little Amronian.

"Is your daddy alright?"

"He says he is going to be fine in a few days. Now, open the bag! I want to see what is inside!"

"What is it?"

"Daddy says it is something for The Chosen Ones to use. It has been hidden in our village for years. I managed to grab it from its hiding place in our house before we had to leave. He knows you're one of The Chosen, and he thought you may be able to use them."

Victoria slowly opened the flap on the leather bag as Windmere and Trakken walked over to watch. Inside the bag was a set of old gauntlets; they were a little rusty and looked like they hadn't seen action for years.

"What is so special about a set of old combat gauntlets?" Trakken asked as he reached out for them, only to jump back in surprise, rubbing his hands.

"Those are not just any gauntlets. Those are The Broken Gauntlets!" Windmere gasped. "I have heard a legend of three weapons that were forged centuries ago, and their purpose was for a Chosen One to wield them and to bring justice and peace to the land. They can only be used by the one who is chosen by The One Above. The Broken Gauntlets are one of the three weapons."

"Like The Empty Sword?" Victoria asked.

"That is another one of the three weapons, yes. The third is called The Servant's Sword, but it has been missing for a very long time. Nobody has any clue where it might be found."

Victoria gingerly reached out with her right hand and grasped the edge of one of the gauntlets. Feeling no pain, she slipped her hand inside and found it to be a perfect fit for her. She quickly pulled them both on and tried a few practice swings. They were just as lightweight as the boots and gauntlets she had received from the blacksmith upon her arrival in that world, but these new ones were rougher and had more jagged edges, and the fingers were tipped with small points, like claws, and there were also small, hooked spikes on the wrists like climbing claws.

"Well, these are different, that's for certain. Thank you, Hannela, and please thank your daddy for me."

"You are welcome," a voice purred softly from behind the group.

They turned around, and there stood the Ripper, his chest and his left eye covered in bandages. Hannela bounded over to him and rubbed her furry face against him, purring like a housecat, but she backed away when he winced in pain. Her black tail drooped and lay on the ground.

"Sorry, Daddy. I forgot you were hurt there."

"It is alright, my little one. Now, you should go play with your brothers. I need to talk to our friends."

Hannela looked back at Victoria, smiled, and quickly rushed away.

"I wanted to thank you for saving my family last night. I am in your debt, and I am truly sorry for what I have done while I was working for that monster," Ripper said quietly.

"I forgive you," Victoria said in a quiet tone. "But I would ask a favor of you."

"And what might that be?"

"To come with me and rescue my brother Steve. He was knocked off of Trakken last night during the retreat, and we think he may have been taken into the ruined city."

Ripper looked at her with sadness in his eyes. "As much as I would do anything to help you, that I cannot do. The ruined city is home to the prisoners that The Shadowed One has taken during his campaign. The whole place is filled with enemies and, even worse, the Unkarian's trained wheelats. I am sorry, young one, there is no possible way for us to enter that city and return alive without a massive army."

Victoria's shoulders dropped and she sank to her knees as she felt the exhaustion and emotion come over her like a wave. She started crying as Windmere picked her up and carried her over to a tent, where Victoria cried herself to sleep, all the while praying for her brother's safe return.

STEPHEN WOKE UP IN a dark room. Besides the stone wall behind him, the other three walls were lined with metal bars that bordered the other cells to his left, while the cell to his right was more like a large pit dug into the ground.

Stephen stood up on his wobbly legs and looked over to his neighbor in the adjoining cell. It was a female Blakmian mercenary much like the ones that had harassed him and his allies on their journey. She was taller than any of the others he had met at just over six feet in height; her wings were a dark grey color, and the undersides of them were white with black spots on both sides. Her tail was grey that faded to black on the tip. The talons on her hands and feet were a glossy black.

She looked up at Stephen and glared at him.

"Some hero you are. Have you saved the world yet? Oh, wait! You cannot, because you are not strong enough, and now you are stuck in here!" she said in a cold tone before turning her back to him.

"Hello to you too," Stephen replied in a similar tone before turning to look into the pit that was to the right of his cell. He peered over the edge and tried to make out what was at the bottom when he noticed eight glowing red eyes looking back up at him. He screamed and jumped back from the bars and against the Blakmian's cell as the huge spider's face appeared at the top of the pit and looked into his own cell.

"I think she likes you," the Blakmian woman whispered into his ear through the bars.

"Precisely why I am going to get out of this place!" Stephen said, spinning around to face the mercenary, who burst out laughing.

"If it was so easy, I would have done it days ago. The only way out is either through that pit or the tiny feeding hatches above us. They keep the wheelat queen in that pit and starve her so that anyone trying to escape will get eaten. The pit borders both of our cells; we wouldn't make it five feet without that thing catching us."

"Just give me some time. I bet I can get out." Stephen began to check the pouches on his sword belt and his pockets.

"I would not bother; they took all my weapons and tools before throwing me in here," the Blakmian retorted as Stephen found what he was looking for and held it up triumphantly.

"They missed my Swiss army knife!"

"A what?"

"It's a tiny tool that has many tools built into it, which can fold up into something you can keep in your pocket."

"So how is that going to help?"

"I...don't know."

"I figured as much."

Stephen began to look around his cell. Besides some loose stones lying around the floor and a wooden bed set into the wall, he really didn't have much to work with. He walked over and looked at the metal bars and found them to be somewhat old and rusty but still sturdy. He then turned to the rough wooden bed and saw it was just made of some wooden poles about an inch and a half in diameter set into the wall.

That's when an idea came to him: he pulled out his Swiss army knife, opened the hacksaw blade, and began to cut one of the wooden poles out of its spot on the wall. Once he had a two-foot pole in his hands, he cut some notches into the sides around the top of it. He then quickly began to look at the loose rocks that were scattered about; once he found one that would suit his needs, he took the laces off of his boots and began to lash the stone to the end of the pole using the notches he cut on the wood to fasten the laces. He could feel the Blakmian's eyes on him while he worked; he hoped that she wouldn't be a snitch and alert the guards, if there were any, to what he was doing. Once he had the stone firmly attached, he swung his newly-created mallet in an arc, testing to see how well the bootlaces held the stone in place.

"I will admit, that is impressive," the Blakmian said quietly. "But how is that going to help us?"

"Watch me," Stephen replied before beginning to hit the bars separating their cells with all of his might. After a few strokes, he could see that the bar was beginning to come loose at the ceiling. He raised the mallet to strike again but was stopped by the Blakmian, who reached through the bars and grabbed the mallet.

"Stop! The guards are here! Hide it quickly!"

Stephen quickly ran over to the bed and sat on the mallet just as a trapdoor in the ceiling opened, and three gritters dropped into each cell. The gritters started searching both cells, and Stephen watched as they looked over at the bar he had loosened. While the gritters looked at the weakened bar from both sides, Stephen looked up, and, to his relief, he only saw a few more gritters above them, and he didn't hear any greatures or Unkarians either.

Now was the time to strike; he slowly reached into his pocket, opened the Swiss army knife's large knife blade, and slowly got up and walked over to the gritters, who still weren't paying him much mind. With one quick motion, he stabbed one in the back of the neck with his knife, killing him instantly. He then quickly attacked the other two, stabbing them both in the eyes and neck.

Once they were dead, he looked over and saw that his cellmate had followed suit and dispatched her gritter trio as well. Before they had time to celebrate, the rest of the gritters dropped into the cells and began to attack. Stephen raced over to the bed, grabbed the mallet he had built, and began to swing wildly at his assailants, while the Blakmian slashed away with her talons.

Soon, all the enemies were dead and lying on the floor. The two warriors looked at each other, trying to catch their breath.

"Nicely done. There will be more on the way soon," the Blakmian said with a grim smile.

"I know. Start pushing them into the pit. I have another idea."

Stephen began to push the dead gritters through the bars and down into the spider's den. He could hear the spider below them begin to dine on their victims, but he really didn't care at this point.

"Once you get them all into the pit, try and cover up the blood with dirt, so it's less noticeable," Stephen said as he began to push the dust and dirt over the pools of grey gritter blood. "By the way, what's your name?" he asked.

"Peregrine," she replied.

"Nice to meet you, Peri. I'm Steve. Now, would you like to get out of here?"

Peregrine frowned and turned away from Stephen. "As much as I would like to, there is no way we are getting ourselves out of this foul place."

"We'll just see about that," Stephen said as he began to finish knocking the bar loose with his hammer. When the top of the bar came out, he caught it before it came free and hit the ground. Just as he began to wedge the heavy bar between two more bars, he heard voices overhead.

"What is all that noise down there? You are not trying to escape, are you?" a greature growled from above the cells.

The hatches opened, and two greatures poked their heads into the cells and looked around.

"Do not try any funny business. We kill escapees on sight," one of them growled before closing the hatches again.

Stephen looked at his homemade mallet in his hand and the bar he had displaced lying on the ground next to him. "Those things really are stupid, aren't they?"

Peregrine sighed, "You have no idea."

Working together, the two prisoners managed to make a gap large enough for Peregrine to squeeze through into Stephen's cell using the detached bar. Stephen held out his hand for his ally to shake, but she pushed it aside.

"Well, I am in your cell, now. What is your next step, genius?"

"We just need to get into that bug's den and escape from there."

"You are joking! That thing will eat us both!"

"Maybe, but she did just have a nice meal of fresh gritter a little while ago. Maybe she will be full enough so that she will ignore us and let us get out through that hole in the roof."

"Well, I guess we should get it over with, then."

The two tested the bars on the side of the cell and found them to be loose. Soon, they had dislodged two bars and were able to fit through the gap.

"Can you carry me out?" Stephen asked Peregrine.

"Carry you?"

"I can't climb to the hole in the roof. I'll need some help."

"So do I. I need a distraction, and you will do just fine," Peregrine said with a smile as she shoved Stephen into the pit. He landed on a pile of loose dirt and looked up to see Peregrine flying above him.

"You can't leave me here!" he shouted as she made her way to the opening.

"That is what they all say. Now, if you will excuse me, I have a bug to avoid. Do me a solid and keep her busy, will you?" she said before blowing him a kiss and quickly flying out of the hole just as the spider leaped up to try and catch her.

Stephen hurried over the edge of the pit and tried to hide behind a pile of bones, hoping the spider wouldn't see him. He saw the spider trying to push her way out, but the wooden roof held firm, and she dropped to the ground again and began to search for him.

Stephen held his breath and ducked down behind the bone pile; he looked for anything he could use as a weapon, as he left his mallet in his cell. He reached out for a large bone when he saw what looked like an old wooden chest partially buried in the dirt.

He quietly pulled it out, slowly opened it, and nearly let out a gasp in surprise. Inside was a small one-handed sword. It was very simple in design with a very small cross-guard and hilt. The blade was clean and in perfect condition, and along the blade was inscribed: "MUST HAVE A SERVANT'S HEART."

Stephen picked it up and felt a wave of energy come over him. He stood up and heard the sound of the spider locating him and rushing towards him. He instinctively closed his eyes and held out his hands as if to try and stop her.

He then felt a hairy thing brush up against his open palm.

He opened his eyes, and the spider had stopped and was gently nuzzling his hand with her face like a cat or dog would do. He looked on in shock as the spider turned around and lowered her large abdomen as if she wanted him to ride atop her back.

Drawing every bit of courage he had, Stephen strapped his sword to his back and climbed onto the hairy beast.

The wheelat queen began to climb the sides of the pit and stopped just below the roof. She looked at him, and Stephen felt she was expecting him to do something. The spider gestured to the old support beams with a leg, then Stephen realized what she was doing.

"You want me to cut them down? Is that it?" he asked out loud.

The spider made a loud clicking sound and angled herself, so he could better reach them.

Stephen pulled his Swiss army knife, opened his hacksaw blade, and began to start cutting away at the beams.

Suddenly, as he was finishing cutting his second beam, a shout rang out from the cells.

"Stop!"

Stephen jumped and looked over to see two greatures had jumped into his former cell and were trying to squeeze through the gap he had left. Knowing he didn't have much time, he turned back to the beam he was cutting to find, to his surprise, he had broken the hacksaw blade off.

"No!" he shouted before pulling his sword from his back and began to wildly slash at the beams and found, again, to his surprise, that it easily sliced through them like paper.

Just as the greatures managed to enter the pit, the monstrous spider lunged at the roof and burst out into the late evening air. Stephen looked around and saw that they were in a large, ruined city and that they were standing on top of what looked to be an old jail of some sort. Gritters and greatures were running away in terror in all directions, as Stephen and his new eight-legged friend started to run across the crumbling rooftops at top speed.

Stephen held on for life as ruined buildings flashed past him. When they came to the top of one tower, Stephen spotted a large group of greatures mustering below them, with spears and bows at the ready. The spider shrieked and started spitting large white globs of silk like a machine gun, and soon, all of the enemies were stuck to the ground, trying to free themselves. The two escapees jumped to the ground and started racing along the streets, making their way out of the city, when they heard a scuffle and someone shouting to their right. Stephen bent forwards and tugged on the spider's head, forcing her to stop.

"Let go of me, you foul creature!" screamed the distinctly female voice.

"That's Peri! Sounds like she needs us to rescue her!" Stephen shouted.

But the spider shrieked and clicked in protest.

"I know! I know! She isn't very nice, but we should help her out!"

The spider clicked again and pointed to the edge of the city with a foreleg.

"Because that's what heroes do!"

The spider clicked and groaned but turned to her right and began to run down the street until they came upon Peregrine being held down by two greatures, while two more giant spiders stood by. Peregrine was covered by the wheelats' silk and was trying to break free from its hold.

Stephen and the spider slid to a stop. The greatures took one look at him and his scary steed and dropped their weapons in fear. The spiders started to attack but were swiftly told off by Stephen's mount, and they backed away.

Stephen was about to jump off to help Peregrine, but she quickly sliced the webbing with her talons. She glared at him and tried to take off, but her right wing gave out, and she tumbled to the ground again.

"Come on! You can ride with me! We'll get out of here together!" Stephen shouted.

Peregrine glared at him again but slowly approached the spider and climbed aboard. The greatures still stood nearby, completely frozen in fear.

"Looks like greature is on the menu tonight!" Stephen shouted.

His spider steed shrieked, and she and the two other wheelats pounced on their helpless prey.

Chapter 15. Too Little, Too Late.

Victoria sat up in her tent, shivering in the cold night air. She thought she heard something moving in the forest.

"It's probably just another animal," she told herself. She had been lying awake for hours now, hoping to hear something, anything, from the scouts Vulant had sent out at dusk. Besides a single report of some unusual activity at the ruined city, nothing had been confirmed to be related to her brother's whereabouts or condition.

That's when she heard two voices off in the distance.

"Dashing through the city! On a colossal spider queen! Through the enemy, we go! Laughing maniacally!"

"Will you just shut up?!"

"Aww, come on! Admit it! It's a catchy tune!"

The first sounded like Stephen...singing...to the tune of "Jingle Bells"? But the other voice was one she didn't recognize.

She grabbed a cloak and her weapons and hurried outside, where she found some guards standing nearby.

"Did you hear that too?" she asked them.

"Yes, commander. One of our watchmen reported some wheelats coming through the forest. We came to stop them, but when we heard singing—" A Kittrian guard responded before he was cut off by a shout from the dark woods.

"Hello, there! Anybody home?"

"Stephen?! Is that you?!" Victoria shouted back.

"Hi, Tori! We were hoping to find you!"

"We?"

Just then, half a dozen dark shapes came out of the tree line and into the moonlight. It was six of the huge spiders and, to the utter shock of Victoria and the guards nearby, Stephen and a Blakmian mercenary were riding on the back of the biggest one of the group. The herd of spiders came within thirty feet of the guards, who raised their spears and swords, ready for an attack.

Stephen slid off of the spider, followed by the Blakmian. Stephen walked over to the spider's head, patted it gently, and the beast returned the gesture by rubbing her face against his. Victoria's jaw dropped in amazement at what she was watching.

"Can I keep her? I already named her Sheila," Stephen asked, looking back at his sister.

"I don't think that would be a good idea," she responded quickly.

"Oh, alright." Stephen turned back to his mount and whispered something to her, and she then clicked loudly. After rubbing her face against him again, she and the other spiders turned around and disappeared into the dark forest. Stephen and the Blakmian walked over to the guards and Victoria.

"Peri, this is my sister Victoria. Tori, this is my escape buddy Peri," Stephen said, pushing Peregrine forward towards Victoria.

"Nice to meet you. I'm sorry if Steve annoyed you," Victoria said.

"You have no idea," Peregrine huffed.

Stephen ignored the comments and turned to the guards. "Could one of you take her to the healing tent? She hurt her wing while trying to escape earlier."

One of the guards led Peregrine, still glaring at Stephen, away, while the others turned back to their patrol and left the twins alone.

"Come on. I'll take you to your tent," Victoria said as she led Stephen away. "By the way, why did you name that thing Sheila?"

"Because that's the name of the big spider in the book series we like, isn't it?"

"That's *Shelob*, silly!"

"Oops. Well, it's too late now, as she responds to Sheila anyway."

The twins talked all of the way back to their tents and were both soon asleep.

The next morning, the area was covered in a thick mist that was rising from the nearby lake.

Suddenly, an alarm went up from the camp.

"Something is coming! Guards! To your stations!"

The twins grabbed their weapons and hurried over, only to find their friends already waiting, their weapons drawn.

"What is it?" Victoria asked as they ran over.

Ripper lifted his head and sniffed the air, his eyes narrowed before he responded.

"Fire Giants," he said grimly.

Suddenly, through the mist, the twins saw a flash of fire igniting and flames forming into the shapes of enormous swords, axes, maces, clubs, and spears. Then, out of the mist stepped giants even taller than the Unkarians at around twenty feet in height. Their skin was dark like volcanic stone, and their armor reminded them of obsidian. Their eyes and mouth glowed a fiery red, and flames covered the edges of their weapons and armor. They marched towards the assembled army and finally stopped within ten feet of the group.

The biggest one in the center stepped forward and spoke.

"I am Vesuvian, one of the seven giant chieftains. I heard there was to be a battle, and I and my warriors are here to lend you aid."

Groman, Galent, Windmere, Ripper, and Vulant stepped forward as well.

"Thank you, Vesuvian. We are most grateful for your help. Please come with us to discuss our battle strategy," Galent said.

The giants extinguished the flames on their weapons, and the six leaders walked away, followed by the rest of the giants.

"Well, I guess we have some more help for when we fight again," Stephen said before turning to his sister, who was starting to shiver. "What's wrong, Sis? Can't take the cold?"

"Don't you feel it? The air is getting colder by the minute!" she retorted before the sound of many paddles pushing the water made them turn towards the lake.

Through the mist, they spotted the shapes of boats made of ice coming across the water. Inside the boats, they could see dozens of small figures holding weapons and ropes. The boats reached the shores, and a figure with a rope and stake jumped out of each boat and soon had it secured to the shore. The rest of the figures then leaped out of the boats and made their way to the twins. They were short, the tallest being nearly four feet in height; their skins were a pale blue, and their long hair and beards were pure white. They wore blue coats and armor, and their weapons, which consisted of swords, war hammers, halberds, and pikes, seemed to be made of pure blue ice.

"They must be the Ice Dwarves," Victoria said quietly, as the small army, numbering nearly a hundred in all, approached the twins.

"Good morning, young ones. I am Frostous, the centurion of this fine group. Where are your leaders? We are here to pledge our allegiance for the coming battle."

Stephen motioned for a Blakmian guard to come over and asked him if he would take the dwarf centurion to where the rest of the leaders were assembled. As they walked away, one of the dwarves walked over to Stephen with a concerned look on his face.

"I hope you know you have a wheelat queen and some of her brood nearby in the woods. We spotted them on our way over, but they were out of range for us to deal with them," he said with a worried tone.

"Oh, I know. That's Sheila. I tamed her in the ruined city and brought her back with me. She and her brood are on our side," Stephen replied with a smile.

The dwarf looked shocked and leaned back.

"What? You trained one of those monsters? How?"

"Easy. I just fed her a few dozen greatures and gritters, so I guess we're friends forever now."

The dwarf stroked his beard in deep thought and then looked Stephen over. Then, he noticed The Servant's Sword hanging on Stephen's belt and Victoria wearing The Broken Gauntlets, with her Tekko-Kagi claws securely mounted on top. His eyes went wide in surprise.

"You are The Chosen Ones! Of course! How could I have not seen it before?" He reached into a large satchel and pulled out six small bottles of a dark blue substance and handed three to each of the twins. "I made these for The Chosen Ones when I heard you had been found. Be careful with them; they are jars of pure ice essence. When the jar is broken, the essence will instantly freeze anything it touches completely solid."

Stephen looked the jars over and then he and his sister placed them into pouches on their belts.

Stephen offered a hand for the dwarf to shake; the dwarf seemed hesitant to accept.

"Are you sure, sir?"

"Yes. I'm sure."

"If you say so."

The dwarf took Stephen's hand with a strong grip and shook it. Stephen felt his hand begin to freeze inside the dwarf's strong, icy grip, yet he forced himself not to flinch and smiled the whole time. The dwarf released his hand and walked away towards the leader's tent.

As soon as he was gone, Stephen started rubbing and blowing on his hand, trying to warm it up again. Victoria just chuckled, and the two of them made their way to the large pavilion where the leaders had gathered.

As the twins got closer, they could hear voices shouting at each other from inside, and they hurried into the pavilion.

There, they found all the leaders in a heated argument; some even had their weapons drawn, and the Fire Giant leader was about to take a swing at Galent, who was not paying attention to his attacker, because he was arguing with the Ice Dwarf leader.

Stephen signaled to Groman, who stood nearby, and the two of them leaped in front of Galent with their swords drawn.

The giant stepped back in surprise, and Windmere slammed her hands down on a map table and shouted.

"Silence!"

Everyone went quiet, and Victoria stepped into the center of the group.

"What is going on here?! I expected better behavior from the leaders of these tribes than this!"

The leader of the Ice Dwarves spoke: "Why are these ruffians here? And why did you allow them to join our army?"

"Because they came here to help. They volunteered themselves to our cause and to try and get rid of the Shadowed One," Galent responded.

"If you do not want to be around us, then leave," the giant said in a huff.

The Ice Dwarf was about to reply when Stephen jumped up onto the map table.

"Stop this, now! If we keep fighting amongst ourselves, we will have no chance of defeating the enemy, who is almost certainly marching towards us and our villages right now. We need to put our differences aside and work together; otherwise, the whole world of Lulandal will be lost."

The leaders murmured among themselves, and Galent, Vulant, and Groman stepped forward.

"Stephen is right! We have no hope of defeating the Shadowed One's army if we do not join together! I have seen what kind of army we are up against; we are heavily outnumbered as we are now! If we can muster our forces and attack now, we may be able to catch the enemy off guard and take the ruined city by surprise!" Vulant shouted.

"How do you propose we take a city with our numbers as they are?" the Ice Dwarf asked.

"We have a small number of Trodontian and Kittrian reinforcements on their way into the camp right now. They have brought the six trebuchets and a dozen ballistas that have been completed at Prariat so far," Windmere responded.

"Vesuvian...Frostous...you both came looking for glory in battle, am I right? I have a plan that may just suit all of our army's talents and skills," Stephen said as he jumped off the map table. "Here is my plan for tomorrow's attack: since they want to fight so much, the Fire Giants and Ice Dwarves will act as the vanguard and attack the city frontally, with the siege weapons giving covering fire. Meanwhile, the Trodontian and Kittrian forces will charge through the woods by the city and attack from the north. Victoria, Groman, my trained wheelat queen and her brood, some volunteers, and I will scale the mountains to the south and attack from there. Since we will strike from three fronts, The Shadowed One will be forced to divide his forces to defend against all three or focus on one and face getting outflanked and crushed. Whichever side is gaining the most ground will try to push through and help the others.

There was a murmur of discussion among the leaders for a few seconds before Frostous spoke up: "Why do you have my people fighting alongside the Fire Giants? We do not need their help. My men are the best my people have to offer!"

At this, Vesuvian folded his massive arms and scoffed. "Is that what you think? I do not care. I and my soldiers are here not just because we want to fight, but because we know that if we do not, *your* army will fall, and the enemy would be at our gates within a month. If I had my way, the entire army would be with us, but the six other chieftains have decided to shore up their defenses and leave everyone else at the Shadowed One's mercy. If you dwarves want to follow your strategy and fight alone, so be it; I and my warriors will follow the plan and, if necessary, will lay down our lives for the good of Lulandal."

Frostous stopped grumbling and looked at his enormous rival. "If that is how you view this battle, then I and my men would be honored to fight by your side."

Vesuvian looked down at the dwarf and gave him a playful shove, nearly knocking him off his feet.

"For Lulandal!" Vesuvian shouted.

"For Lulandal!" The other leaders echoed.

After a rousing cheer, the leaders began to plan for their attack, which was to take place the next morning. Stephen and Victoria stood nearby when they each felt a gentle hand on their shoulders. They turned around and saw the familiar face of Elder Gilder of Areiop.

"I need to speak to you two and Groman. There is something you three need to know," he said before turning around and walking out of the tent.

Stephen and Victoria motioned for Groman to follow them, and they exited the tent and saw elder Gilder walking northwards, up a steep, forested hill, and out of the camp. The three Chosen Ones followed him, and soon, they found Elder Gilder sitting on a rocky ledge, looking down at the camp. The twins walked over to him and sat down next to Elder Gilder on his right, while Groman sat on his left.

"I have come with news for all of you. Groman, your sister sends her regards, and she told me to tell you she will be awaiting your return in Areiop. Stephen and Victoria, I have different news for you. When Geltian told you about The Great Story, he had forgotten one important part. I would have told you upon your return to Areiop after your first victory over the raiders, but The Shadowed One was moving too fast, and I was unable to talk to you then. I am here now, and I want to explain something to you."

"What is it?" Stephen asked.

"While you are indeed chosen, you are not 'the' chosen. Your duty here is to help Groman bring peace to the land. The Great Story says that when the three work together and find the three, the three will become one, and The Chosen One will destroy the evil," Elder Gilder explained.

"I'm not sure I understand. Is that why The Shadowed One kept taunting us that we couldn't defeat him?" Victoria asked.

"That is all that I know. But what I think it means you three need to work together and find three things."

"We did find three weapons during our time here," Stephen said. "Do you think that they are the 'three' that the story talks about?"

"Show me," Elder Gilder responded.

Stephen and Groman drew their swords, while Victoria held out her gauntlets.

"Bring them together," Elder Gilder urged.

The trio held their weapons close to each other, and all three of them started to notice a dim golden light beginning to emit from each of them. The light grew brighter and brighter as they came closer to each other, but when they were about to touch, they heard a loud noise coming from the camp below them.

They pulled their weapons back and stared through the trees. They couldn't see anything at first but then they noticed something moving through the bottom of the valley below them.

It was an army; the largest any of them had ever seen, and it was marching towards their camp.

"He's here!" Stephen shouted.

"And he brought his entire army! He outnumbers us five to one!" Groman echoed.

"That doesn't matter! We need to get down there and ready for battle!" Victoria shouted. "How are we going to get there in time?"

"I gotcha covered," Stephen said with a smile before putting four fingers in his mouth and whistling loudly. Within minutes, a chorus of loud clicks and screeches could be heard, as the wheelat queen Sheila and her five spiderlings raced over towards them. As soon as they came close and stopped in front of the group, Stephen leaped onto Sheila.

"Hop on! They'll get us there long before the enemy arrives!"

Reluctantly, the others chose a spider and climbed aboard their hairy steeds. Soon, they were racing along at top speed through the trees.

As they hurried down the hillside, one thought continued to echo in Victoria's mind.

This is it. This is going to be our last battle.

Chapter 16. Fighting

"What is the plan, Stephen?!" Groman shouted as the small spider-riding group raced down the steep slope towards the camp.

"The enemies are a few miles away yet. My original plan should still work. We just need to get to the camp in time to prepare!" Stephen shouted back as his spider steed leaped over a fallen tree. "We just need to alert the army and grab our gear before we start our part of the plan!"

Within ten minutes, the group arrived at the camp. The commotion caused by the giant spiders quickly brought out the tribe leaders, who stared in shock as Stephen brought his own spider to a stop.

"The enemy is approaching! They are less than ten miles away right now! We need to get the siege weapons ready for defense, and we need to execute the battle plan and cut them off, now!"

Chieftain Galent quickly galloped away, shouting orders to his troops, while Elder Gilder quickly, but shakily, dismounted from his spider and yelled for the Kittrian soldiers to prepare for battle. Windmere, Trakken, and Saralia galloped over to Groman and the twins.

"They are attacking, now?!" Trakken shouted as he skidded to a stop.

"Looks like it. They must be mad about the trouble I caused in their camp yesterday," Stephen said.

Suddenly, they heard a familiar screech overhead, and Vulant and some of his archers swooped down and hovered above them.

"They outnumber us over four to one!" he called down to them.

"Are you counting gritters as equal to one soldier in that ratio?" Stephen shouted back.

"If I did, it would be over eight to one. And that is not the worst of it!"

"What now?!" Victoria shouted.

"There is an entire division of Unkarian troops! The Shadowed One is no longer holding back! We face his entire army!" Vulant responded.

"Are there any reinforcements coming?!" Groman shouted.

"A few small armies are coming from the west, but there is little chance they will make it here in time."

"I see. Well if this is going to be our last battle, let's take as many of them down with us as we can, so they don't pose as much of a threat to the rest of Lulandal," Stephen said before standing on the spider's back and cupping his hands around his mouth. "Vesuvian! Frostous! Are you ready to stand your ground and hold them off?!" he shouted at the two leaders, who were still standing by the pavilion entrance.

"The enemy will burn in battle!" Vesuvian shouted.

"We will freeze them before they can do any damage!" Frostous called back.

"You will most likely see the heaviest fighting there! Are you sure you want to do this?!" Stephen called out again.

"It will cost what it will cost," Frostous replied.

"We will not move for anyone!" Vesuvian roared as he ignited his massive sword.

The two leaders hurried away to ready their troops as some Kittrian soldiers ran over, carrying the armor belonging to Groman and the twins.

"Elder Gilder said you would need this," one of them panted as he ran over.

"Thank you," Groman said calmly as he pulled on his chest plate and helmet. He looked over at Stephen, who was strapping on arm and leg guards. "This is it, is it not?"

"You mean we either win this fight, or we die trying?" Victoria responded as she pulled on a thick leather shirt.

"That's the plan. If we don't slow that army down or at best stop it, then the rest of the land doesn't stand much of a chance," Stephen said as he pulled on his helmet and raised the visor. "Right now, the only thing standing in the way of a complete takeover is us. We are going to stop that army, whatever it takes." He held out his hand towards Groman, who gripped it in his leather glove.

"Whatever it takes," Groman repeated.

Soon, the trio and the six spiders were racing to the south, trying to outflank The Shadowed One's army. Within half an hour, they had reached the mountains on the south side of the valley. They began to climb up the steep rocky slope.

They soon came to a ledge, where they could look out over the entire valley. They saw the fire giants and ice dwarf armies arranged in a "v" formation in the center of a large clearing with the giants at the center and the dwarfs at the sides. Suddenly, they saw The Shadowed One's army burst from the tree line on the east side of the clearing and charge towards the defenders. The Ice Dwarves moved their arms and formed spiky ice shields in front of themselves. The Fire Giants ignited their weapons and braced themselves for an attack.

The enemy army picked up their pace, with a massive swarm of gritters taking the lead. When they reached the outer dwarves, they were funneled towards the waiting giants, who began to burn away at the tiny creatures as they tried to escape but were quickly cut off by the Ice Dwarves, who attacked with their ice weapons or froze the enemy in place before smashing them to pieces.

The next wave of gritters seemed to falter, but the row of greatures came up behind them and forced them to move, only to get the same result.

Now, it was the greatures' turn to try and break the defensive line. As they began to charge, Stephen saw large stones flying through the air and smashing into the oncoming enemies.

"There're the siege weapons!" Victoria cheered.

"That line could hold for a week!" Groman shouted.

But as the trio cheered, they saw a large group of Blakmian archers fly up from the woods and attack the dwarves and giants, pelting them with arrows. The defenders quickly retaliated; the dwarves formed larger shields, and the giants began to literally spew fire from their mouths. But the Blakmians were too far away and easily dodged the attack.

The greatures began their own attack at the defensive line and slowly began to force their way in. The defense began to dissolve into a mess as allies and enemies became locked in heavy combat.

Suddenly, the twins watched as Vulant and his Blakmian army rose from their hiding places in the forest, attacked the enemy archers, and began to drive them away. But Stephen noticed that the enemy Blakmians weren't just retreating; they were moving to cover their flanks. And a small group was coming towards them.

"We need to move, now!" he shouted.

Just then, the spiders began spitting globs of webbing at the approaching Blakmian attackers, dropping most of them. However, one began to fly higher out of the spider's range and began quickly firing its arrows at the small group, as they tried to find cover on the rocky ledge. Before the enemy could let off five arrows, a black and grey streak came rocketing down from the sky at blinding speed. Before the enemy archer could react, two taloned feet sank into his spine and crushed it. The enemy archer let out a squawk of surprise before going limp in the talons of his killer.

Stephen looked up to see who their savior was, only to find it was Peregrine.

"I knew you would need some help! I did not think it would be this bad!" she mocked as she tossed the dead Blakmian aside.

"Thanks for the help, Peregrine!" Stephen shouted.

"Stephen, look!" Victoria cried.

They all looked over and saw that the defensive line was beginning to falter but then they saw the Trodontian army, carrying the Kittrian army on their backs, come out of the northern side of the clearing and quickly smash into the enemy's right flank.

"Now's the time for our attack!" Stephen shouted as the group began their charge down the mountainside and towards the enemy's left flank.

As they swiftly approached, they saw a group of gritters and greatures, who weren't even looking in their direction.

"For Lulandal!" the trio shouted as they descended on their enemies.

Soon, they were locked into battle. Peregrine darted in and out, slashing away with her talons, and Groman and Stephen chopped through anything they could with their swords. Victoria leaped off her spider and began to cut into the enemies with her claws, all the while the spiders were pinning down gritters and greatures alike with their webbing and devouring them with grim efficiency.

The small engagement seemed to be in their favor when they heard a roar coming from within the enemy's ranks. Stephen looked up to see three Unkarian soldiers, wielding huge maces and clubs, charging towards them. He and his spider steed wheeled about to face the oncoming threat and charged at the attackers.

As Stephen and his spider neared the lead Unkarian, Stephen reached into the pouch on his belt and felt the three cold jars of ice essence the dwarf had given him. The spider started spewing her webbing, pinning the largest Unkarian down and encasing him in a sticky cocoon, while the other two were too fast and dodged the incoming globs of silk. When they were less than ten feet apart, the lead Unkarian swung his mace in a downward arc. Stephen watched as time seemed to slow down, and the mace connected with his spider's head, knocking her into the ground. He felt himself being catapulted into the air as the spider went down.

As Stephen flew through the air over the Unkarian, he pulled out one of the bottles and threw it down at the Unkarian's mouth, which was wide open in mid-roar. After clearing the first Unkarian, and still in mid-flight, Stephen swung The Servant's Sword at the second Unkarian's neck and managed to cut its head clean off with one stroke. Stephen tumbled to the ground and spun around to see his handiwork. The first Unkarian had turned a bright blue and was frozen solid, and the other Unkarian's headless body slowly slumped to the ground.

Victoria ran over and helped Stephen up.

"Did you seriously just take two of those things down in less than a minute?" she asked as she pulled him to his feet.

"I guess I did. The third one is all yours. Sheila got him with her webs before...." Stephen's voice trailed off as he looked over at where his spider was, only to see its lifeless body lying crumpled on the ground. "I will make them pay! Every last one of them!" he shouted as he grabbed his sword and shield and continued his attack.

Victoria turned to the last Unkarian, who was still trying to get out of his web prison. She raced over with her claws, ready to finish the job, when she heard a muffled sound coming from within the cocoon.

"Please, no kill Tiny. Tiny no want to fight anymore."

"Very well. I accept your surrender. Stay there, and I will send someone to help you eventually," she said.

She heard a loud sigh come from the mass of webbing.

"Thank you. Tiny will repay nice girl later."

Victoria turned back to the battle at hand and rejoined Groman, Peregrine, and Stephen with his two remaining spiders, as they pressed their attack into The Shadowed One's army.

After about fifteen minutes of fighting, they came to a clearing, where they found a large group of armored greatures waiting for them. The warriors raised their weapons and attacked.

The battle seemed to be going well when Peregrine took off into the air and looked behind them.

"We have more coming in from behind us! We have been cut off!"

Soon, the battle turned into a fight for survival, as more and more greatures and gritters swarmed into the clearing from every side.

The warriors were nearly out of strength when they heard the thunder of hooves rapidly approaching. Within seconds, Windmere, Trakken, Saralia, and a large group of Trodontian soldiers raced into the clearing and quickly cleaned up the remaining enemies.

"I see we made it just in time!" Windmere shouted.

"Thanks for saving my skin again!" Stephen shouted back as he climbed onto Trakken's back. Victoria got onto Saralia, while Windmere helped Groman aboard.

"What happened to your wheelats?" Trakken asked.

"We ran into some Unkarians. They killed my spider queen, and the rest of her brood soon followed," Stephen said sorrowfully.

"I am sure they fought nobly. Now, let us finish this fight!" Windmere shouted as she and the rest of the Trodontians took off at a gallop back into the fray.

The battle went on for what seemed like hours. The allies would beat back The Shadowed One's forces, only for another, larger, wave of enemies to take its place. Soon, the allied army was beginning to falter, as their numbers continued to drop after every engagement.

Then, just after they managed to drive another wave of enemies back, the battlefield became silent. The allied army picked themselves back up and looked in the direction of the enemy, only to see a solitary Unkarian carrying a white banner approaching them.

"Are they going to surrender?" Groman asked hopefully.

"I doubt it," Windmere said. "They have every advantage here. Why surrender when you can just crush your enemy in one blow?"

The Unkarian walked into the space between both armies and raised his voice.

"My lord, The all-powerful Shadowed One, says he is tired of this needless fighting and slaughter. He would like to make you an offer."

"What kind of offer?" Groman asked.

"For the three Chosen Ones to meet him in combat at the old temple to the south. Winner takes all."

"So he wants to get into a fight with just the three of us?" Victoria asked.

"He wants to be the one to personally crush your pitiful lives under his feet," the Unkarian messenger said.

"We accept!" Groman quickly shouted.

Stephen and Victoria looked at him in surprise.

"Are you insane? We'll be walking into a trap for sure!" Stephen whispered.

"If this is the only way to prevent more bloodshed, then I am prepared to take that risk," Groman said solemnly.

"You have made the correct choice. My lord will be waiting for you at the ruined temple. Bring only yourselves," the Unkarian said before turning back into the enemy's ranks.

"Come on," Groman said as he slid off Windmere's back onto the blood-soaked battleground.

Stephen and Victoria joined him and began to walk to the south.

They soon approached a line of gritters, but when they reached the line, the gritters parted and allowed them to pass through. Soon, the trio were surrounded on all sides by enemies but was still allowed entry.

Eventually, they came to a large stone structure that was mostly in ruins. As they neared the rubble, they saw several Unkarian warriors standing guard around the place. Victoria stopped and held Groman and her brother back.

"Groman, are you sure about this? If this is a trap, and it most definitely looks like it is, there is very little chance we will be walking away from this one."

Groman turned to face his companions and sighed.

"This is my destiny; this is what I was chosen for. You are part of the chosen as well. However, I will not force you to sacrifice your life. If you want to go back to our allies, I think I can hold them off long enough for you to escape."

"I'm going with you. We will fight together, and if it comes to it, we will fall side by side," Stephen said firmly.

Victoria looked at the two men with a grave face.

"We have the weapons that were made for us. The whole land is depending on our success." She paused, taking a deep breath. "I know it seems selfish, but I admit I am scared one of us won't be walking away from this."

Stephen hugged his sister and then looked her in the eyes.

"Victoria, I promise I won't let anything happen to you, and I will try to protect myself as well. But I am prepared to do whatever it takes to end this threat and protect our friends. If things turn south, run as fast as you can. Groman and I will stay until the end."

Victoria slowly nodded, tears flowing down her face, and then together, the three Chosen Ones entered the ruins, ready for the battle that lay before them.

Chapter 17. Fulfillment

The Chosen Ones entered the ruined temple and saw they were in a very large stone room that seemed to be larger than even the great hall of Prariat. The roof had seemingly collapsed decades ago and since rotted away, leaving no trace of it and allowing the light of the setting sun to pour in. The walls were covered in intricate carvings that had been worn away by time and partially covered by moss and dirt. Some of the stone blocks had fallen off the wall to the floor and lay on the ground. The floor was mostly covered by grass and moss, but what little of the stone floor that was still exposed was composed of faded mosaics and white marble tiles. There was a stone altar at the far end of the room.

The huge figure of The Shadowed One stood by the altar, with his back towards the three warriors.

"So you have come at last. I admire your courage, coming to face me even though you have no hope of winning," he said as he turned to face them, The Ruler's Sword in his hand and his shield at the ready. "Because of that, I will grant your friends a swift death."

He turned towards one of the walls and shouted.

"Kill them all! Then, march on Areiop! I want to crush that city and burn it and its people to the ground!"

The trio heard a chorus of roars and shouts as the soldiers raced away.

"No!" Groman shouted as he lunged at The Shadowed One, swinging The Empty Sword.

The Shadowed One easily blocked it while turning his shield to face Victoria, who was leaping towards him with her claws at the ready. Victoria bounced off the shield and tumbled to the ground, while Groman and The Shadowed One kept their blades locked.

Stephen tried to sneak around to the Shadowed One's left and slash at his ankles, missing them by inches. The Shadowed One lashed out with his left foot and kicked Groman away, then turned his attention to Stephen, who tried to block his attack with his sword but found that his massive opponent was simply too strong. He instead deflected The Ruler's Sword into the mossy stone floor. Victoria was on her feet within seconds and slashed at the Shadowed One's right ankle, her claws barely scratching the exposed flesh. The Shadowed One swatted her away with his shield just as Groman lunged at him again, this time trying to drive the Empty Sword into his opponent's chest. The Shadowed One deflected the attack with his arm guards, pulled The Ruler's Sword from the earth, and swung it at Groman's chest. Groman jumped up to dodge the attack, but as the sword was mid-swing, The Shadowed One twisted his wrist, causing the flat side of the blade to collide with Groman's legs, sending him spinning into the dirt, where he lay in a daze.

The Shadowed One raised the edge of his shield, ready to bring it down on Groman's body like a guillotine, when Stephen and Victoria lunged towards it and, with every bit of strength they had, managed to block it with their weapons.

"Foolish children. I would have given him a swift end. Now, it will have to be the painful way," The Shadowed One said with an evil smile before raising his shield and swinging his sword at the pair, who ducked to avoid the blade.

"We need to keep him off Groman. Split up! We'll be harder to hit!" Stephen hissed as he went to the Shadowed One's left side.

Victoria went to his right, and the twins prepared to attack the Shadowed One's legs, hoping to bring him to his knees, where they would be able to reach his vulnerable head and neck more easily. The Shadowed One loosened the chains on his shield and started swinging it around him, forcing the twins to keep back at a distance. The Shadowed One then started swinging the shield flail in a different arc so that it started to get nearer to Groman's body with every rotation.

Stephen noticed that The Shadowed One's back was exposed, as the shield was flying higher behind him rather than in front of him. He began to move towards him slowly, raising his sword for another strike.

"You think it will be that easy?" The Shadowed One asked mockingly.

Just then, he turned the angle on the shield, and Victoria saw that it was going to hit Groman on its next rotation. Time seemed to go in slow motion as she moved in front of the shield, raising her gauntlets in front of her chest to try and take the hit from the shield. She could hear her brother screaming for her to get out of the way as he swung his sword at The Shadowed One's leg, cutting deep into the monster's flesh. Then, she saw the shield swing around The Shadowed One's head and come at her at an awkward angle. As she watched the large piece of metal coming towards her, one thought came to her mind.

I'm ready.

The impact of the swinging shield shattered her claws and sent her flying backward towards one of the fallen stones. Her back hit the top edge of the stone, and she felt a sharp pain in her spine before everything went black.

STEPHEN WATCHED IN horror as Victoria stepped in front of the swinging shield.

"No, Tori! Don't do it!" he shouted as he slashed at The Shadowed One's left ankle. The blade swung true this time and cut deeply into the monster's flesh, causing a roar of pain from The Shadowed One as his left leg gave way under his weight.

But to Stephen's terror, the shield kept going around The Shadowed One's head at a different trajectory and collided with his sister.

He watched as Victoria was flung across the room from the impact and landed on the edge of a large stone. A sickening crack echoed around the room, and even The Shadowed One looked up at Victoria's unmoving body. The shattered Tekko-Kagi claws and the special gauntlets had fallen off Victoria's hands and lay on the ground in front of her.

A twisted grin came across The Shadowed One's face.

"You are next," he growled as he stood up again, and his ankle healed.

"You *monster*!" Stephen screamed as he felt the rage overcome him and he attacked with every bit of strength he had left. Adrenaline pumped through him as he swung his sword wildly, trying to cut The Shadowed One as much as he could. The sword had little effect, however, and Stephen saw the shield in the air once more, this time swinging for his head. Stephen ducked and swung his sword at the connecting chain with all his remaining strength.

He heard metal snapping and watched as the huge shield was cut free from the chains around The Shadowed One's wrist and flew into the stone wall, knocking a large portion of it down. Stephen glanced over to where the shield had landed in the wall for a split second, and when he turned back to his opponent, he saw the left arm of The Shadowed One inches from his face. The blow knocked the sword and shield out of his hands and sent Stephen sprawling onto the ground, knocking the wind out of him.

Stephen tried to push himself up but collapsed in exhaustion. He turned his head and could see Victoria's limp body, still lying against the stone. Tears began to run down his face and into the mossy floor.

"I'm sorry Tori, I failed you, I...I couldn't protect you," he whispered softly.

The Shadowed One kicked The Servant's Sword away and slowly walked over to Stephen.

"Yes, you did fail your sister. Now, you get to die knowing that all of your friends will join you and your sister because of your failure," The Shadowed One taunted. "It is a pity; you had no chance since you did not listen to what the story really said. Only when the three become one would you have any chance of defeating me."

The Shadowed One raised his huge sword and prepared to bring it down onto Stephen's body.

"Now, you die," The Shadowed One said as he brought the blade down towards Stephen's neck.

Stephen closed his eyes and braced for the blow, but he heard the clash of metal against metal.

He opened his eyes to see Groman on his feet again, managing to block The Shadowed One's blow with The Empty Sword mere inches from his face.

"You forgot about me," Groman growled, his face set in a look of grim determination.

The Shadowed One tried to force the blades downwards towards Stephen, but his evil grin turned to a look of surprise when Groman kept the swords from moving. Stephen looked at The Empty Sword just inches from his face and saw the engraving on the tip: "A TRUE LEADER."

Suddenly, it all made sense to him.

"Groman, put my sword inside yours and use Tori's gauntlets!" he shouted as Groman managed to lift the two blades and force The Shadowed One to take a step back.

"What?!" Groman shouted at him as The Shadowed One attacked again. The two large blades clashed in the early evening light.

"Remember what happened when we held them together this morning? The three need to become one! My sword is just small enough to fit inside the gap in your sword, and you can wear the gauntlets!" Stephen shouted as he slowly pushed himself to his feet. He looked over to where The Servant's Sword had landed and rushed over to it, picking it up and looking at the engraving that ran down its blade: "MUST HAVE A SERVANT'S HEART." He looked at the Shadowed One and Groman, who were still locked in combat. He frantically looked for a way to get the sword to Groman when he saw a large piece of stone that had fallen off of the old wall. He picked it up and hurled it at The Shadowed One's head. The stone hit its mark, and The Shadowed One turned to look at who had just attacked him. He forcefully shoved Groman away and menacingly strode towards Stephen, who quickly tossed The Servant's Sword at Groman. The sword landed on the stone floor with the hilt sticking up. Stephen looked at The Shadowed One, who was beginning to run towards him. Stephen summoned every last bit of strength he had and ran to his left towards Groman, who was busily grabbing the gauntlets and putting them on.

"Get the sword!" Stephen screamed as he sprinted away from The Shadowed One, who was fast approaching him.

Groman lunged for The Servant's Sword and picked it up.

"Hurry! Put it inside The Empty Sword!" Stephen shouted.

Groman gently placed The Servant's Sword into the gap in The Empty Sword. At once, there was a blinding flash of golden light.

Stephen blinked rapidly to try and adjust his vision. When he could finally see, what he saw took his breath away. There stood Groman, with the gauntlets on his hands and a sword that had been filled. The gap in The Empty Sword was no longer visible, nor was The Servant's Sword; the two blades had merged into one. The sword and gauntlets were glowing with a gilded light.

Stephen heard a laugh come from behind him. He turned and saw the Shadowed One was standing right behind him.

"You may have solved the riddle, but it will not save you," The Shadowed One said as he swung The Ruler's Sword at Stephen, who ducked but was caught off guard by the fist that came after the blade.

Stephen landed on the ground in a sitting position and watched as The Shadowed One turned his attention to Groman, who took one look at the monster and disappeared. The Shadowed One laughed.

"Your last friend has abandoned you. Just as I planned. I have been playing you this whole time, you see. Every battle, every victory, and every loss has all been a part of my master plan to bring you to me. I knew that even if you figured out that ancient story, your friend, the only one who could use all three weapons, was too much of a coward to actually fight."

He stepped over to Stephen and lifted his chin up with the tip of his blade.

"I have won," he said with his evil grin.

Suddenly, the sound of metal cutting into flesh was heard, and blood spurted from the back of The Shadowed One's legs. He sank to his knees with a roar of frustration and pain.

"You have come back to fight after all!" he jeered.

"You know, I think I have it figured out!" Groman's voice echoed around the ruined temple, seemingly coming from anywhere and everywhere. "I could never fully disappear with The Empty Sword, but that was only because it had not been filled yet. Now, there is no chance you will see me coming!"

Another slash, and a large cut appeared on The Shadowed One's right arm. The wound healed quickly, and The Shadowed One rose to his feet again, looking all around him, trying to figure out where Groman was. Another strike and deep gash appeared on The Shadowed One's left leg.

"That was for the people you murdered!" Groman shouted.

The Shadowed One roared again as another cut appeared on his right leg.

"That was for the villages you plundered!"

Another hit tore a large chunk of The Shadowed One's chest plate off and cut deep into his stomach.

"That was for Falamore!"

The Shadowed One swung The Ruler's Sword wildly, trying desperately to hit his invisible assailant. Suddenly, Groman appeared next to The Shadowed One, swinging The Empty Sword down onto The Ruler's Sword. The blades clashed, but this time, The Ruler's Sword shattered like many pieces of glass. The Shadowed One looked at the broken hilt in shock as Groman lunged at him.

"And this..." Groman said as he swung his sword at the monster's neck, cutting deep into the exposed flesh. "...is for Annie!"

Blood poured from The Shadowed One's wounds as he sank to his knees, coughing.

Groman stood in front of him, his sword raised and ready to strike.

"Finish him!" Stephen shouted.

Groman lowered his blade. "Surrender, and I will spare your life," he said firmly.

"Are you crazy?!" Stephen shouted over The Shadowed One's coughing. "He'll just escape and come back to get you and your sister!"

The two warriors watched as The Shadowed One's coughs became laughter.

"He is right, you know. You cannot spare me; I will break out of whatever hole you put me in, and I will hunt you down. I will torture and kill everyone you love, starting with your sister. And I will make you watch!" The Shadowed One laughed maniacally.

Groman's blade remained at his side.

"I will find your little sister, and I will do more than cut off her legs. This time, I will make her end a slow and painful one! I..." The Shadowed One taunted.

Groman covered his ears and screamed. "Stop!"

"I will start by cutting off her hands and then slowly work my way up the arms to the body, then I—"

The Shadowed One's words were cut off by Groman screaming and The Empty sword slicing through his neck.

The Shadowed One's face twisted into an evil smile as his head fell off his body and landed on the ground.

Groman stared at his blood-soaked sword in shock before dropping it to the ground and sinking to his knees.

"I killed him," he whimpered quietly.

"You did the right thing. He would have only come back to haunt you and Annie in the future," Stephen said as he walked over to Groman and put his hand on his shoulder.

"I hope so."

Suddenly, the two men heard a soft moan come from where Victoria was still lying.

"Tori!" Stephen shouted as he and Groman hurried over to her still-unmoving body. Groman gingerly reached out and felt her pulse on her neck; a look of shock came over his face.

"She is alive but only just! We need to get her to a healing tent right away!" he said.

"But isn't it a bad idea to move her if her back is injured?" Stephen asked.

"Yes. We need to find something flat we can carry her on."

The two men quickly looked around for something they could use as a stretcher. Suddenly, a glint of light reflecting off something metal caught Stephen's eye. He hurried over and saw the Shadowed One's shield, still embedded into the fallen wall.

"Help me pull this out!" he shouted as Groman rushed over after he sheathed his sword. Together, the two of them pulled the heavy shield out and carried it over to Victoria. They gently moved her onto the shield, making sure to support her back to keep from making any injury worse. Then, they carried Victoria on the shield between them, and they made their way out of the ruin.

When they came out of the ruins, they saw that the sun had nearly set, its remaining light coming over the mountains to the west. However, they saw that there was a large army of Unkarians, greatures, and gritters waiting for them.

The two men gently placed the shield on the ground, and Groman pulled The Empty Sword from its sheath on his back and held it high in the air.

"Your king is dead! Surrender, and we will be merciful!" he shouted towards the enemy army.

A wave of murmurs came from the line of enemy soldiers, and one of the Unkarians stepped forward and raised a huge spear.

"If you have indeed killed our ruler, our orders are to kill you on sight!" The Unkarian shouted as the rest of the army raised their weapons.

Groman held his sword high, the blade glowing in the dim light, while Stephen drew a dagger from his belt and pulled the remaining jar of ice essence from one of Victoria's pockets. The two men faced down the entire enemy army, side by side.

"Are you ready, my friend?" Groman asked.

"Whatever it takes, right, Groman?" Stephen responded.

The lead Unkarian hurled the spear at the two warriors, who both prepared to dodge the attack, but to their surprise, nothing came.

The Unkarian turned around to see Vesuvian the fire giant holding the spear. The Unkarian drew a dagger the size of a one-handed sword and went to attack the giant but received a knockout punch to the jaw in return.

Suddenly, the whole area became a battleground once more as the battered, but still very much alive, allied armies rushed in and attacked the remainder of The Shadowed One's forces.

Stephen and Groman stood over Victoria's limp body, doing their best to keep her from being trampled in the chaos. Abruptly, they heard two screeches overhead. Stephen looked up and saw Peregrine and Vulant flying over them.

"Vulant! Peregrine! We need your help!" Stephen shouted as loud as he could.

The two Blakmian warriors didn't seem to notice and continued on their warpath. Stephen's shoulders slumped in defeat.

Groman held his sword over his head and closed his eyes. Suddenly, a brilliant beam of golden light burst from the blade and rocketed skyward for a few seconds. Vulant and Peregrine wheeled about and turned to see what had caused the light. They both dove towards the three Chosen Ones, landing beside them.

"You need to get Tori to the healing tent, now! Her back was injured during the fight with the Shadowed One!" Stephen exclaimed through tears.

Vulant and Peregrine didn't say a word but quickly picked up the shield between them and took off into the air once more, flying towards the camp.

Once they knew Victoria was safe, Stephen and Groman turned their attention back to the battle and joined the fray. Despite their and their friends' exhaustion and injuries, they fought on, and the enemy was beginning to falter.

Soon, the last of the enemy forces had either surrendered or were lying dead on the battlefield. By the time the three moons were above the mountains, the battle was over. The allied army took the Unkarian prisoners back to their camp for interrogation while sending the greatures and gritters away under heavy escort.

Upon their return to the camp, Stephen and Groman were waiting outside the healing tent, when chieftain Galent walked over with three Unkarian prisoners. Two of the Unkarians looked at Groman with faces of despair and sorrow, while the third only glared at them with all the hate and malice he could muster.

"Shall I have them sent back under the Black Peak?" Galent asked.

Groman thought for a few minutes.

"Please do not banish us again. We only followed The Shadowed One because we wanted to be out in the world again. He promised us that we could see the sunrise once more and be a big part of the land like our ancestors were in the past. I cannot speak for my brothers, but I am sorry for what we had done to you and your peoples," one of the Unkarians pleaded.

Groman started to reply but was cut off by Saralia slowly walking out of the healing tent. Stephen looked at his Trodontian friend; she had an impressive black eye and some scratches from the day's fighting, but what concerned him the most was the look of dread and sorrow on her face.

"Stephen..." she said quietly.

"Please don't tell me that Victoria is..." Stephen said, fighting back tears.

"She is alive. Vulant and Peregrine got her here just in time. But..." she replied, but before she could finish, she was cut off by Victoria's screams from inside the tent.

"My legs! Why can't I feel my legs?!"

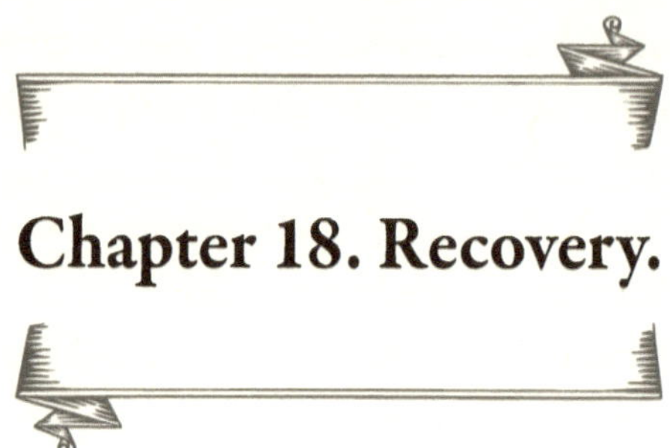

Chapter 18. Recovery.

Stephen felt like an ocean of emotion had just hit him as he sank to his knees and closed his eyes. "No...no...no!" He slammed his fists into the ground and started to sob. Victoria's pained cries still echoed in his ears as he broke down.

He heard Saralia's hooves as she rushed back into the tent with Groman close behind her. Soon, Victoria's screams of pain and confusion quieted down, but Stephen remained on the grass still in shock from what he heard. He then felt a strong hand grasp his shoulder and Groman's calm but sad voice as he knelt next to him.

"She is sleeping, now. We gave her as much of the pain-blocking herbs as we dare, but I am afraid her back has been too seriously injured. I...I am so sorry. There is nothing we can do. Your sister will never walk again," Groman said quietly.

Stephen held his face in his hands and cried some more. Groman sat next to him and gently laid his arm on Stephen's shoulder.

The two men wept softly for a few minutes until they heard a Unkarian start shouting.

"Wait! The little girl hurt?! Tiny can help little girl! Let Tiny help!"

Stephen looked up and saw that the largest of the Unkarian prisoners was trying to break free from his bonds, while the third Unkarian was holding him back. "Quiet, you nitwit! She got what she deserved for killing our king! Besides, what do you think you can do to help her? You are nothing but a stupid half-wit who does not even know how to fight!"

Stephen walked over to the three Unkarian prisoners and looked at the one who was calling himself Tiny.

"Tiny, as much as I appreciate your wanting to help my sister, I'm afraid it is impossible. Your healing abilities only work on yourselves. Unless you can somehow give your ability to Victoria, I'm afraid there is no hope," Stephen said sorrowfully.

"Tiny can do that! Tiny can!" Tiny tried to talk, but the third Unkarian had managed to break his bonds and had clapped a large hand over Tiny's mouth.

In a flash of metal, Groman leaped forward and slashed at the evil Unkarian with his sword, cutting the monster's arm off with one swing. The Unkarian howled in pain and fell backward onto the ground, where he was held down by several soldiers.

Tiny looked at the Unkarian in shock and then turned back to Stephen.

"Tiny can heal sister. Tiny's mother taught Tiny that long ago, before exile, Unkarians were great healers. Then, Unkarians became proud and tried to rule world, then exile. Tiny's mother taught Tiny how to heal others. Tiny pledged to help little girl after little girl spared Tiny's life in battle. Tiny want to repay sister by healing her."

"Are you sure about this?" Groman asked.

"The only thing I am sure of right now is that if there is a chance for my sister to walk again, I will take it. Tiny, if there is anything you can do to help her, please do. Even if it only eases her pain." Stephen walked behind Tiny, drew his dagger, and cut the ropes that bound Tiny's wrists. Tiny then pushed past Stephen and walked into the healing tent, with Groman and Stephen right behind him.

Saralia and the other healers looked up in surprise when the large Unkarian entered the tent, but Groman motioned for them to step away from Victoria's cot.

Tiny stopped for a moment when he saw Victoria's limp body lying in front of him.

"Shadowed One do this?" he asked quietly.

"Yes," Stephen replied in a whisper.

"Tiny sorry Tiny fought for monster."

"I forgive you, Tiny. Can you please try to help my sister?"

Tiny stood over Victoria, put his hands together, and closed his eyes. He then began to mutter a prayer while slowly rubbing his hands against each other. Stephen watched in amazement as Tiny's hands began to faintly glow with a blue light. Tiny, still muttering the prayer, then gently laid both of his huge hands on Victoria's body. He held his hands there for what seemed like an eternity but was only a few minutes. Tiny then opened his eyes and moved his hands away.

"Tiny done all Tiny can do. Up to One Above now," he said with a weak smile before passing out and falling to the ground beside the cot, shaking it and all the beds around it.

Stephen and Groman checked to make sure Tiny was alright before they looked at Victoria. She was still sleeping, but Stephen felt that she looked more peaceful than when he had first seen her.

"I hope that Tiny did it," Stephen whispered to Groman as they left the tent.

"I am praying to The One Above that he did," Groman replied.

The two men walked out into the night air and found Windmere had joined chieftain Galent in waiting outside, the Unkarian prisoners having been sent away.

"How is she?" Windmere quietly asked.

"She's sleeping peacefully for now. An Unkarian called Tiny tried to heal her, but we don't know if he did any good," Stephen responded.

Galent raised an eyebrow. "I see. Well, we still have the issue of what to do with the Unkarians. They could be considered enemies and executed for what they have done to so many people. We could just exile them back under the Black Peak and take extra precautions to make sure another Shadowed One doesn't rise from beneath it."

"No. Enough blood has been shed today. There will be no killing," Groman said firmly.

"So exile again?" Galent asked.

"If I could share my opinion really quick?" Stephen cut in. "In my world, there was once a huge war where nearly the entire world was caught up in the fighting. In the end, the countries that won forced one of the countries that started the war to pay for everyone's debts. This caused that country to get into so much debt that the people looked to someone, anyone, who promised that they could fix their problems. They elected a leader who was a vile, hateful, and evil man. That man killed millions of people and started another war, a war that was bigger than anyone had seen and has seen since. The good guys won in the end, but millions of people paid the price with their lives."

"And your point is?" Galent asked in a confused tone.

"Sometimes, when we seek to punish our enemy, we only create new ones instead. Sending all the Unkarians back into exile may be a humane way to deal with them, but you heard one of them saying they only wanted to see the sunrise over the mountains again. Permanently banishing them again may not be the best course of action," Stephen replied.

The other warriors nodded in agreement and then turned to Groman.

"How about this? We send them back but have some trusted guards watch them. Those who seem like they are good enough to leave the peak will be allowed to return to their old place in the world and become a part of Lulandal's society once more. Those who only harbor malice and hate will remain in their self-imposed exile until they change their ways," Groman said confidently. "But we will not tell them of this plan, or else some may put on an act in order to leave. We will let their true natures show who is worthy to be released. And I would start with releasing the Unkarian who tried to help Victoria. He has shown his true colors this night."

The two Trodontians nodded in agreement and then looked behind Stephen and Groman. Stephen saw their faces go from puzzlement to shock in a few seconds; he wondered what was up when he felt a hand tap him on his shoulder.

He spun around to see Victoria on her feet and looking better than when they had left their great aunt's house. She grabbed him in a bear hug, and he readily returned the embrace. He felt the warm tears running down his face one more. But this time, they were tears of joy and not sadness.

That night, after the celebration of Victoria's recovery, the entire army slept well, knowing that their families, friends, and their homelands were safe once more. Stephen wasn't sure he could sleep after seeing his sister on her feet again but was out the moment his head hit the pillow.

The next morning, the twins were greeted by the returning slaves who had been freed by Ripper and his Amronian friends, who had raided the ruined city during the previous day's battle. Then, the whole happy company began the long journey back to their homes.

At the end of two long days of traveling, the twins could see the southern border of Areiop through the forest pathway. As the victorious army approached the gates, they heard a loud fanfare of trumpets and horns come from within the city. The gates slowly opened, and a large procession of Kittrian, Blakmian, and Trodontian people marched forwards towards the army. The soldiers began to break ranks and run to meet their loved ones. Then, another trumpet blast caused the crowd to separate, and the three Chosen Ones saw four Trodontians carrying an ornate litter with its curtains drawn, marching towards them.

The four Trodontians came over to Groman, turned to their left, and set the litter down. A voice came from inside the litter.

"Come forth, chosen hero of Lulandal."

Groman gave Stephen and Victoria a puzzled look, then turned to approach the litter. He came to the curtain, and before he could pull it away, two arms reached out and wrapped around his neck, and Groman pulled back in surprise, bringing Annie with him. She was clinging to his neck and laughing while Groman looked at her in surprise. Then Groman embraced his little sister, the two of them crying for joy. The Trodontians picked up the litter and carried it back inside the gates. The army began to make its way inside the city. At the rear of the army, Stephen and Victoria walked side by side, and Groman followed close behind them, carrying Annie the whole way.

That evening, there was a feast unlike anything the twins had ever seen. Practically everyone they had met and befriended was there. The entire village square had been turned into an outdoor banquet hall, with tables and benches scattered everywhere and colorful lanterns hanging from the trees and banners that had been strung over them. A group of musicians from all the different villages and cities provided the whole banquet with a beautiful serenade. Stephen, Victoria, Groman, Annie, Galent, Vulant, Windmere, Trakken, Saralia, and all the other heroes were seated at their own table on a raised platform. All of them were dressed in fine attire and happily feasting on the fantastic food.

Then, Elder Gilder and Elder Geltian stood up from their table and motioned for everyone to be quiet. The entire party became silent as Elder Gilder began to speak.

"I would have never thought that this day would come. To see the old evil defeated and the world at peace at long last is a great blessing to me. And we have these people to thank!" The party cheered and applauded for a few minutes before being silenced again. "Because of their service, we of the united tribes would like to honor those who helped our cause. Stephen, Victoria, and Groman, please come forward."

The three Chosen Ones got up and walked over to the elder. Elder Geltian pulled out a decorative wooden box and set it on the table as they approached. Groman knelt before the elder, and the twins followed suit.

"Groman of Fruniet, you have done your people an incredible service. The story of your kindness, your skill in healing, and your determination in battle will be passed down for many generations to come. For this, we award you the Medallion of Heroes, an honor very few in our history have earned," Elder Gilder said as Elder Geltian pulled out a shiny gold medal on a scarlet ribbon and placed it around Groman's neck. "Stephen, we would have lost without your bravery in battle and your cunning tactics. For this, we also give you the Medallion of Heroes, as a small token of our gratitude." Elder Geltian produced another medal identical to Groman's and placed it around Stephen's neck. "Victoria, for your kindness to the peoples of every tribe and your willingness to sacrifice everything to save our land, we give you the Heroine's Pendant. We have only given this award to one other person in our history. This is a small token of thanks for everything you have done for this world."

Geltian gestured for his wife, Velien, to stand up, and he handed her a necklace with a large gold pendant in the middle. Velien draped it around Victoria's neck and smiled at her.

The three Chosen Ones stood up and began to bow to the Elders when Elder Gilder stopped them.

"No, it is not you who should be paying respect to us," Elder Gilder said before he and the other elders bowed before the trio. Soon, all the Kittrians, Amronians, and Blakmians were bowing, with the Trodontians giving their left arm salute with their heads bowed.

Stephen and Victoria blushed and smiled, while Groman looked over at his sister, who was still seated in her wheelchair, grinning from ear to pointed ear.

The trio returned to their places at the table, and the celebration resumed.

Soon after they had finished eating, the twins noticed that the tables in the center were being cleared away, and a large open area was being created. Annie started bouncing in her seat with excitement.

"They are going to dance! Come on, Groman! Dance with me!" she exclaimed happily as she wheeled herself over to the dance floor.

Groman stood up and looked over at the twins.

"Are you coming?" he asked teasingly.

"We'll let you dance with Annie for a bit before we cut in," Victoria said with a laugh.

Groman, Annie, and some other partygoers all lined up in the center, facing each other. Then, the music changed to a lively tune, and the dance began. Groman and Annie backed away from each other and came together, and Groman walked down along the line, while Annie wheeled along by his side in her wheelchair. They then backed up again and turned around. The men stood and clapped while the women twirled for a few seconds, their dresses flowing out around them. Annie was doing her best to keep up with Groman and the other partygoers, but she sat still in her chair instead of spinning. After the ladies had stopped their spinning, the next pair of dancers came up and changed partners.

Groman was surprised to see Victoria and Stephen walking up to them.

"Mind if we cut in?" Stephen asked with a smile.

"I would be honored," Groman replied. Before he realized it, Victoria had taken Annie's place, and Stephen was wheeling a giggling Annie away. The dance resumed, and Victoria did her best to keep up with Groman, who, even after she stepped on his foot, still seemed happy.

After spinning for a bit, Victoria stopped and pointed behind Groman.

"What's that?"

Groman turned around for a second and looked behind him. Seeing nothing, he turned back to where Victoria was, only to find her missing. He looked around and spotted Victoria back in her seat. She smiled at him and pointed behind him. Groman turned, and a second later, he saw Annie appear out of thin air, walking towards him, her bright silver dress nearly glowing in the lantern light and two beautifully engraved silver prosthetic legs appearing from under the edge of her dress. Annie stopped in front of Groman and gave him a huge smile. Everything around the two siblings seemed to fade away as Groman looked on in shock.

"Surprise!" Annie shouted with the biggest grin she could manage. Groman's eyes began to water then he gave his sister a huge hug, with tears of joy once more running down his face. The dancers continued around them as if they hadn't yet noticed the happy reunion in their midst.

But Stephen and Victoria watched on from their seats, a joyful look on their faces too.

"You know, Tori, I never thanked you," Stephen said quietly.

"For what?" Victoria asked.

"For dragging my sorry hide out into the forest on that cool summer day. To think we would have never experienced this if we hadn't gone exploring that day boggles my mind."

"You're welcome. And thank you for standing by me through it all. We never could have made it without each other. I'm thankful to have you as my brother."

The twins hugged again as they watched Groman and Annie joyfully dancing together under the moonlit sky. Soon, the brother and sister rejoined them at the table, and Annie ran over to the twins.

"Come on! Dance with me! Groman says he is too tired to dance anymore!" Annie pleaded.

"I'd like to, but I'm not very good at it. I'd hate to step on your toes," Stephen replied with a smile.

Annie responded by kicking Stephen in the shins with her new legs.

Stephen winced and bent down, rubbing the bruise. Victoria and Groman laughed for a bit before helping Stephen up.

"Alright, Annie. I'll dance with you for a bit," Victoria said with a laugh.

Groman and Stephen sat back down at the table and watched Victoria and Annie along with the rest of the dancers as they spun around the dance floor.

"She planned the whole thing with you, am I correct?" Groman asked.

"I can neither confirm nor deny," Stephen replied with a wry grin.

Groman chuckled and leaned back in his chair, sighing with contentment as the rest of the partygoers enjoyed themselves.

After a few more joyful hours, the banquet died down, and everyone went to bed. Victoria laid awake on her mattress, looking out of a window at the trio of full moons that illuminated the night sky. She sighed to herself, thinking about the adventure she and her brother had experienced the past few weeks: *I wonder if we'll ever see this world again after we go home.* She hoped they would be able to have more adventures here with their new friends. But that was out of their control; they couldn't come back here whenever they wanted, could they?

The question echoed in Victoria's mind as she fell asleep.

The next morning, after a huge breakfast, the twins met up with their friends in the town square. Windmere gave both Stephen and Victoria a bone-crushing bear hug, Trakken shook their hands, and Saralia gave Victoria some of her special herbs in a little leather pouch.

"Just in case your brother gets himself hurt again," she said with a smile and a wink at Stephen, who rolled his eyes.

Just then, Chieftain Galent trotted over with two large wooden boxes in his arms.

"A token of the Trodontian people's gratitude for your service to our city and land," Galent said as he handed one box each to Stephen and Victoria.

Stephen quickly opened his and let out a gasp of delight as he saw a beautifully-forged hand-and-a-half sword inside. The sheath and sword belt were inside the box as well as a gold horseshoe pendant. Victoria found a nearly identical one-handed sword and pendant in her box, but where Stephen's sword had a large deep red gemstone set in the center of the hilt, she had a brilliant white diamond-like stone that sparkled in the daylight. Galent then saluted the twins, and after a quick hug from Saralia and another round of tearful goodbyes, the Trodontians galloped away into the sunrise.

Stephen had his new sword in its sheath strapped to his back within a few minutes, whereas Victoria looked at her new blade a little closer, admiring the handiwork that must have gone into it.

Then, Groman and Annie walked over to them. Annie had swapped the decorative silver prosthetic legs she had worn the night before to a sturdy but still ornately carved wooden pair and was happily skipping along by her brother's side.

"Do you think we haven't noticed?" Victoria said to Annie with a wry smile.

"Noticed what?" Annie giggled.

"That you're nearly a head taller than when we first met you," Stephen replied.

"Well, that is the benefit of getting new legs. I can make myself as tall or as short as I please!" Annie replied, and the whole group burst into laughter.

"Seriously, though, how can you walk so well on those solid wooden legs?" Stephen asked.

"They are not completely solid; there is a metal spring in the ankle that gives me an extra 'spring' to my step!" Annie replied. "I watched the blacksmith work for two days on these, so I know how they work."

"Very nice. Now, as sad as I am saying it, we need to be getting back home," Groman said with a slight frown.

The twins and Annie nodded, and together, they set off on their journey back.

As they walked, they reminisced on the adventures they had been on and the battles they had fought, filling in gaps where one of them had not been present. Stephen told them of his daring escape from the prison on the back of the giant spider. Victoria talked about her and Saralia's mission to Tredut and their rescue of Annie. Annie told them stories of her and Groman's time in their home village. Groman remained quiet during all of the storytelling.

Around noon, they came to the village of Fruniet and stopped for a small feast the Kittrians had made for them. The villagers were much kinder to the twins after their last visit, as the traitorous elder had fled after The Shadowed One's defeat.

After they had eaten, they resumed their journey once more on the tree-lined tunnel. It was nearing sundown when they finally came to the village of Tredut, where they found the villagers were waiting for them. Elder Geltian and his wife walked over to the travelers and hugged the twins.

"We are so thankful you came to our village. I hope that we may see you again someday," Geltian said with a smile.

"Me too. I hope we can have many more adventures in your fantastic world," Stephen replied.

"Now, before you go, we have some gifts we would like to give you," Velien said with a grin. Another villager walked over with two cloth bundles and handed them to the twins. "You will find the clothes you were wearing when you arrived in our world inside as well as some of our legendary Kittrian green tea and a surprise for each of you. Do not open them until you are back in your own world. And you will find one more surprise waiting for you on the trail."

Victoria ran forward and hugged Velien again. Then, the four travelers began the final leg of their journey to where Stephen and Victoria had stumbled into their world.

As they walked through the moonlit tunnel, Victoria noticed Annie seemed to be sniffing the air, then whispering something to Groman, who looked around and smiled. That's when the twins noticed a sweet fragrance unlike any other, wafting towards them.

"What's that smell?" Stephen asked.

"Moonflowers! And a lot of them!" Annie said excitedly as she picked up her pace and ran ahead of the group around a bend in a trail. The others hurried to follow her and saw the walls of the tunnel seemed to be growing small bulbs that covered nearly every inch of them.

"They are going to bloom any second now!" Annie squealed with excitement as the bulbs continued to get bigger and bigger. Soon, bits of bright blue light seemed to be coming from inside the flowers, and small cracks began to form. Suddenly, the bulbs began to burst open into beautiful, blue five-petaled flowers that glowed with a brilliant azure light. Within seconds, the four friends were surrounded by thousands of glowing flowers, as the tunnel was completely covered in the fantastic foliage. Stephen stood still with Groman and Annie, while Victoria was turning in circles, looking all around her, trying to take in all of the beauty at once.

"They must have planted these just before we came. They normally would not plant the flowers in the pathways, as it would attract gritters, but now that the threat is over...." Groman's voice trailed off as Annie put a finger to her lips.

"Just let them enjoy it," she whispered.

After a few minutes, the group began to walk down the lighted tunnel, stopping every now and then to enjoy the sight before them. Then, Stephen noticed a large opening cut into the tunnel to his right.

"That is our way out," he said quietly before facing Groman and Annie.

"I guess this is where we say goodbye," Victoria said, with tears beginning to form in her eyes.

"Not quite," Annie said as she stepped forward and hugged her friend. "That pendant that you received last night...I do not know if this is true, but...." Annie pulled out an identical pendant from her cloak. "I have heard stories about those who have these and their being able to hear whoever has the pendant's other."

Victoria pulled out her pendant and looked at it. It had the four crests of the allied tribes engraved into the golden metal: a horseshoe with crossed swords, a tree with a longbow at its base, a large feather with an arrow in an "x" formation, and a cat's eye with a small dagger behind it. Annie lifted her pendant up and held hers against Victoria's, and Victoria felt a strange rush of energy flow through her hand when they touched. Groman held out his medallion, and Stephen did the same. Copying what Annie and Victoria had done, they pressed them together, getting the same result.

"I do not know if they actually will let us contact you, but you never know," Annie said with a slight smile. Victoria hugged Annie again, while Stephen and Groman shook hands.

"You know, Groman? I never got to see your new sword; do you mind pulling it out one more time?" Stephen asked.

Groman pulled out the large blade and held the handle out to Stephen, who looked a little unsure of taking it.

"Trust me," Groman said with a smile.

Stephen slowly reached out for the handle and grasped the sword with his right hand. To his astonishment, he could hold it without being hurt, and it was actually rather heavy; he had to use two hands to hold it properly. He looked over the complete blade and saw the engraving that ran down the length of the sword: "A TRUE LEADER MUST HAVE A SERVANT'S HEART."

"How did you make this thing look so light?" he asked in surprise, holding the handle out to Groman, who easily took it held it in one hand.

"Odd. I never even noticed the weight," Groman said as he swung it around and then placed it back into its sheath on his back.

"Probably because you are The Chosen One," Victoria said with a smile.

"Well, Tori, we probably should be getting back. Great Aunt Belinda has probably called the cops by now," Stephen said as he started to make his way towards the opening in the tunnel wall, only to be stopped by a big hug from Annie.

"Promise you will come back if we need you again?" she pleaded.

"As much as I don't like to make promises I can't keep, if you need our help, and we can come back, you can be certain we will," Stephen said.

With that, the twins exited the tunnel. When they were a short distance away, they looked back and saw the silhouettes of Groman and Annie against the blue light of the moonflowers waving at them. The twins returned the wave and continued to push their way through the thick forest trail.

After nearly half an hour of hiking, they came out into a large clearing, where they saw the back of their great aunt's house and the old barn she used to keep her horses in during the winter when she raised them.

"Let's put our stuff in the barn. I wouldn't want to try and explain why we showed up in Kittrian clothes and carrying swords," Stephen suggested.

The twins ducked into two empty horse stalls and opened their bundles that had their earth attire. Stephen heard Victoria let out a little gasp.

"What is it, Tori?" he asked in concern as he pulled out an ornate Kittrian dagger in its sheath.

"It's the dress I got from Velien on our first night in Lulandal!" came her response from the adjoining stall.

"I knew she would give it to you! I got a really nice dagger from Geltian!"

Soon, the twins were back in their earth clothes, and, having left their otherworldly attire and weapons in a safe hiding place, they went back outside.

As they walked over to the front porch of their great aunt's house, Victoria placed her hand on the pendant she had under her shirt. She couldn't bear to part with it and had brought it with her, hoping her great aunt wouldn't notice.

Stephen knocked on the front door and got an immediate response.

"Steve? Tori? That had better be you!"

"It's us, Great Aunt Belinda! Can you open the door?!" Victoria shouted.

Within seconds, the door was thrown open, and the short muscular frame of their great aunt burst through and was hugging them both.

"Where have you been all day? I was nearly about to call the police!" she said as she pulled away from the twins and dragged them inside and closed the door. "Alright, out with it! Where did you go? And what did you do?" she asked with a wry smile.

Stephen and Victoria both gave her a confused look.

"What do you mean?" Stephen questioned.

Belinda swiftly reached out and grabbed the chain on Victoria's pendant and pulled it out of her shirt. Victoria gasped in surprise and tried to reach for her pendant, but her great aunt held it away from her.

"Well, you've met some strange folk; I know that for certain. How were things in Lulandal?"

The twin's jaws dropped to the floor in surprise.

"How do you know about Lulandal?!" Stephen asked in shock.

"Oh, I spent a long time there nearly thirty years ago, when I was around your age. Didn't anyone mention Belinda the Brave?"

"No. Nobody did," Victoria responded.

"And here I helped put the Golden One on his throne in Altimi. You'd think they might remember that."

"Wait! The Golden One? Falamore's father?" Stephen asked.

"He had a son? I'm glad to hear he was able to settle down and have a family."

"How did you wind up in Lulandal?" Victoria asked.

"As you probably know, I am the youngest of a very large family. That's how I can be your great aunt but still younger than your mother. Well, I was left out of a lot of things when I was your age, and I started to explore the woods behind this house. One day, I found a tunnel made of trees, and I followed it, only to find myself in that world. The rest is their history. Now, did you bring anything from there back with you? Please tell me you brought some Kittrian tea here. A friend of mine there made the best tea I ever had. Ah, Geltian, such a goofy fellow, but he was nice enough. You know, it's been almost thirty years since I've had any of that tea, and I'd give anything to have some again."

Once again, the twins' jaws hit the floor in surprise, but their great aunt seemed equally taken aback by their reaction.

"I take it we have a lot of things to talk about tonight. Why don't you go get your things and bring them inside, while I get a little something I brought back from my adventure there?"

The twins hurried out to the barn and started to gather up their weapons and Kittrian clothes. Stephen even strapped his gifted sword to his back despite Victoria's protests.

As the twins stepped inside the house, they were greeted by their great aunt wielding a large two-handed greatsword of her own, made out of a black metal with red gemstones decorating the hilt. "Won this from a fire giant in a duel. He used this thing with one hand as a dagger."

After comparing blades, the three of them sat down with some freshly-brewed Kittrian tea, and the twins told their great aunt Belinda the whole story of their adventures in Lulandal long into the night, with much laughter and a few tears.

Chapter 19. Only the Beginning.

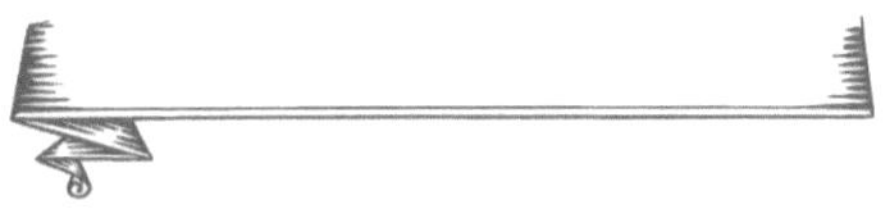

Nearly a week had passed since the twins' adventure in Lulandal. Their lives had seemingly settled down to normalcy when their friends Jack and Dani came over for the weekend. Victoria and Dani were sharing a room that Friday night and talking about Dani's recent trip to camp and the archery lessons she had taken while there. Victoria didn't dare tell her friend about her recent adventure, as she knew Dani would just call her crazy.

After talking for a while, Dani got up from her mattress on the floor to go use the bathroom. While she was gone, Victoria lay back on her pillow and closed her eyes.

"Tori."

The voice made Victoria quickly sit up in bed and look around.

"Tori!"

Victoria quickly lifted her pillow to reveal the pendant she had received at the end of her adventures. She noticed a dim blue glow emanating from it. She gingerly lifted it up and watched in awe as bright particles of blue light poured out of it and took the shape of her Kittrian friend Annie in the middle of her room.

"I did not expect for this to actually work. But I can see you in my room!" Annie's voice echoed.

"I can see you too! This can't be real!" Victoria said in astonishment, leaping off the bed and walking over to her friend.

"I wish I could be as excited as you. We need your help. There is something brewing outside of Lulandal's borders that we cannot handle on our own. We need you, Tori."

"I don't know if we can even come back!"

"Please try. I do not know how much longer we can hold out."

Just then, Annie's form looked to her left and let out a short scream before her form disintegrated into the blue particles and disappeared into thin air. Victoria looked at where the form of her friend had been standing then stared at her pendant in amazement.

Then, something in her peripheral vision caught her eye, and she looked up to see Dani standing in the doorway with a look of pure shock on her face.

"What was that?" Dani asked in surprise.

Before Victoria could respond, Dani walked into the middle of the room.

"Better question, who was that? And when do we go?"

About the Author

Hi there! I'm Jonathan Zobel, the author of this book. I'm a big history nut and I grew up reading many many books throughout my childhood and teen years and I've always enjoyed a good story. I was homeschooled by my parent's all the way through high shcool and I attended Faith Baptist Bible college in Ankeny IA for two years, graduating with an AA. I was a playwright for a few years before I shifted to writing books.